In the Dead of the Night

Cayce stopped to listen to the faint lap of water against the boat. How long would it take for a man's body to come to the surface? If it were weighted, if it were sucked down deeper and deeper into the muddy bottom, it might never be found.

He had to go to John's cottage. Perhaps, just perhaps, John had returned.

He found his way again along the grove path. Leaves thrust through the fetid darkness and brushed his face. When he reached the cottage he called out, but there was no answer, and everything—even the clouds of dead insects that seemed to inhabit the silent cottage with their own whispering little lives—was the same.

He turned out the lights and went slowly back along the path. He had to see Dodie. Maybe now she would be willing to share with him that memory that had seemed to her so frightening and significant.

He had almost reached the Howard house when he heard Dodie scream from somewhere in the deep blackness . . .

Also by Mignon G. Eberhart

Published by
WARNER BOOKS   *forthcoming

MIGNON G. EBERHART

ANOTHER MAN'S MURDER

WARNER BOOKS

A Warner Communications Company

All the persons and events in this book are entirely imaginary.
Nothing in it derives from anything that ever happened.

WARNER BOOKS EDITION

Copyright © 1957 by Mignon G. Eberhart
All rights reserved.

This Warner Books edition is published by arrangement with
Random House, Inc., 201 East 50th Street, New York, N.Y. 10022

Warner Books, Inc.
666 Fifth Avenue
New York, N.Y. 10103

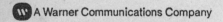 A Warner Communications Company

Printed in the United States of America

First Warner Books Printing: July, 1983

Reissued: February, 1988

10   9   8   7   6   5   4   3

The long double line of Australian pines stood like black sentinels against the greens of grove and lake. Cayce turned the rented car into the lane between the trees. The shady driveway was slippery as always with brown needles. The Australian pines had not changed, except to grow thicker. Midway through the long tunnel of twilight he reached the gate, which was open and sagging, held up with a weather-beaten rope. Cayce frowned when he saw that. Through the gaps of the tall Australian pines he caught glimpses of the east grove. This lay between the driveway and the lake.

The lake itself made a deep curve; the house stood within the curve. The shortest way between his house, Blanchards, and the Howard place at the west, or John Tyron's little cottage, snuggled into the lowland east and beyond his own place, was by boat across the lake. Through the grove, too, he caught a flash of the flat, sparkling lake. The lake itself could not have changed either in six years, although so much had changed.

Driving out from Tampa he had felt that he was in a new land, following new and unfamiliar roads, past whole towns which in his memory had been mere clusters of filling station, post office, general store, and were now thriving, lively settlements shining with new pink and white and yellow houses —all with television antennae springing above them, and laden with patches of purple bougainvillaea and coral-colored honeysuckle. Everything seemed so new and so glittering and clean and prosperous that only when he saw some old landmark, like the church at Val Roja or the glossy green acres of grove lands, had he a sense of homecoming. He came out of the shadowed driveway and turned the car into the circle that went around the house.

He stopped beside the great clump of Melaleucas. The house stood before him, long and beautiful in its lines—and unpainted, shabby, and smothered with unpruned vines. He got out of the car, looked around him.

The roof needed mending; a gutter pipe sagged away from the house; shutters here and there were askew, hanging by rusty hinges. The long veranda, which crossed the entire front of the house, was obscured by a heavy growth of bougainvillaea which dropped great purple garlands along it. A chimney was crumbled at one corner. Cayce took a long breath;

5

he was determined to control any emotion such as anger that might threaten him. He turned and walked across the lawn halfway to the lake.

The lake was long and irregular, bordered by groves along the Howard place and his own, and pasture land and great live oaks directly across at the Burke place, but there were also patches of lowland and irregular inlets which went back into the swampland. He could not see John Tyron's cottage standing on a patch of lowland which was in fact a part of Cayce's land. His father would have wanted him to see John but he couldn't, he didn't dare, take the time.

Nearer at hand there were further evidences of neglect. The once green lawn was patched with brown. The huge crescent of camellias was patchy too, for plants had died and had not been replaced. The driveway itself, which made a circle before the house, was now an uneven sandy track, its edges weed-grown. And everywhere vines and shrubbery had grown like lush green fingers trying to snatch the land back to its old-time, primitive state. Only the lake was the same, and even there, in front of the house, the reeds and rushes had encroached upon the land, as if they sought to creep nearer and nearer.

All around him the groves made glossy, green curtains. He looked in the direction of the old fishing pier, but he was too close to the trees at that point; the green bank of the west grove intervened; he wondered if the fishing pier, too, had fallen into disrepair. What had the judge done with the money?

Apparently no one had heard his car arrive; that, or no one was in the house. He was taking a chance of course, expecting the judge to be at home. But in his mind he had covered that contingency; if the judge were not at home he would find him, nevertheless, in Val Roja or Suncas City or wherever he was, have that short interview, and still make the evening flight back to New York.

It was going to rain. He knew Florida storms. He glanced at the sky and it was a soft and pearly gray; the rain wouldn't last long.

He wouldn't even enter the front of the house. That would be too much like homecoming. He went along the path at the side of the house, toward the study and estate office. The judge had taken over the study; he'd taken over everything, as if it belonged to him. The shrubbery was so thick here that he had to push his way past it. A huge raindrop struck his forehead.

He came to the French door of the study, and the lamp on

6

the desk was lighted so its green shade glowed brightly within the dusky room. That, too, was as familiar and loved as the house, the soil, the warm and humid air, the very smell of his own land. Then in the circle of light on the desk he saw a man's plump hands, idly playing with a pencil. He couldn't see the judge's face.

It was suffocatingly hot; Cayce's collar seemed too tight, his Northern clothes too heavy and sticky. He slid out of his coat. There was a soft rustle as the first flurry of rain struck the foliage beside him. He opened the screened door.

The hands froze for a second and he knew that the man behind the lamp had lifted his head with a jerk. Then he half rose and stared at Cayce above the green-shaded light.

"Cayce—why, Cayce! This *is* a surprise!"

The screened door closed with a little rasp behind Cayce. "You said you wanted to see me."

"Well—but—my dear boy," the judge said. His mellifluous voice sounded a little uncertain. Then he pushed himself to his feet and put out his hand. "Welcome home."

There was nothing for it but to shake hands with him. Cayce crossed to the desk, and the judge's hand was moist and flabby. Neither prolonged the clasp.

"Sit down," the judge said, "sit down. Well. It's been a long time."

"Six years," Cayce said, and sat down in the old leather-covered armchair. It had always been there; the maroon color of the leather was only a little more faded and cracked. Everything in the room was intensely familiar to him; it was as if the green-shaded lamp, the glittering, dark glass doors of the bookcases, the core of the house itself had invisible but strong threads attached to his heart. The light glimmered on an orange in crystal and gold which had belonged to his father. He wouldn't look at it and he wouldn't succumb to the pull of all those tough threads.

He looked at the judge and the judge eyed him warily. They were like two enemies reconnoitering each other's strength. The judge had changed very little. He was a big man, stooped and paunchy but big; his face was brown but flabby with its sagging checks and chin. He was nearly bald, so his heavy reddish eyebrows seemed very prominent; he had small darting eyes deeply lined, and an oddly fine and delicate nose, almost a woman's nose set in that gross face. "Well," he said again, "you didn't write."

"I got your letter, so I decided to come." Cayce eased his legs out, crossing one ankle over the other. He put his coat down and loosened his tie.

"I see. . . . It's very hot—starting to rain," the judge said, observing Cayce's gesture, as he observed everything. He put one hand out toward a silver bell on the desk. "Something to drink?"

"No thanks. I've got to get back to Tampa—back to New York."

The red eyebrows lifted. "Tonight?"

"Yes. I've got a job. But you know that."

A flicker of relief crossed the judge's face. "Of course, but—tonight? Why, it's been so long. You'll want to see the place, see Blanche and Roddy."

Cayce shook his head. "I've got to leave in half an hour." There was no use in waiting for the judge to come out with whatever he had to say; he was like a wily old fisherman when it came to waiting for his prey to make the first move. Cayce said, "What's it all about?"

The judge blinked. He picked up the pencil again and eyed it. "Interest—affection." He seemed to debate and said, "It's time you made a visit home."

Cayce, who knew the judge so well—too well, recognized the evasion for what it was. "You meant something more specific than that. You said you wanted to see me. What about?"

The judge lifted his red eyebrows. "Don't you think you ought to have let me know where you were all this time?"

"You knew. Your letter was directed to me."

"But you didn't tell me, Cayce."

Curiosity flicked Cayce. "How did you get my address?"

The judge smiled and put his flabby but oh so tenacious fingers together neatly. "Not from you," he said with an air of sad reproach. "You treated me very badly, Cayce. Me and your Aunt Blanche. Left here without a word, in the night, six years ago. And never a word from you since then. You didn't write to John—and you took your father's place with John. You were important to him, surely you knew that. Why, you never even wrote to Midge. She felt it, Cayce. She felt very hurt."

"She was engaged to Roddy . . ." Cayce began, on the defensive in spite of himself. He checked his own words and said, "I suppose you got my address from the Army."

The judge's smile was fixed on his face, as if a mischievous spirit had painted it there. "I am your next of kin. Blanche and . . ." He frowned. "My dear boy, you have not even inquired about her."

Blanche and the judge, brother and sister, were like two

8

pieces of the same person so far as Cayce was concerned. He said stiffly, "I'm sure she is well."

The judge shook his head. "How hard you are, Cayce!"

The silken, ugly taunting was beginning. Cayce's hands tightened on the worn leather arms of his chair, and in the same fraction of a second he thought, I was a boy then, vulnerable and lonely; nothing the judge can say now can touch me. But the things the judge could do, or fail to do, had the power to wound. He said, "What about the groves?"

The smile on the judge's face became a little less smug. "Oh, well, now—things haven't been so prosperous for us, you know."

Cayce's long body tensed. "Not prosperous! Why, the whole country around here looks as if there's been a boom. All the new building, the new roads, the young groves . . ."

"It's not all velvet. For an old man like me it's been hard. You left home just as you were reaching the age where you might have been of some help."

There was truth in that. "I couldn't have stayed," Cayce said flatly.

To his vague surprise the judge smoothly agreed. "I realize that you had to make your own way. You obviously like your job. I wouldn't ask you to give it up. But this is your home. Blanche and I did everything we could for you. Your father left you in our charge. We did our best. You never loved us, either of us. You never gave us your respect or confidence. You were always rebellious and resentful. . . ."

Cayce had heard that too many times in his boyhood. He said, "Is Zack still here?"

Zack was the grove superintendent and had been the grove superintendent ever since Cayce's father had bought the place, built his house, brought his young wife there to live. The judge tapped the desk with one pudgy finger and said, "Yes. Zack's still here."

"How many grove men have you?"

"Two."

"Two! A place like this needs at least five."

"Wages are high. You don't know anything about that. Expenses for everything are high. I can only do my best."

The rain was beating down hard now upon the house, the groves, the lake. How well Cayce remembered the sound of the rain, like a swift drum! Soon it would slacken off, become light and pattering, and then abruptly stop, and the sun would come out. "But receipts for the grove must be on an equal level," he said.

9

The judge moved back in his chair—the chair that had belonged to Cayce's father. "Not what you might think. We have our troubles. Frost, insect pests, rust . . . I don't like your attitude, Cayce. I've worked hard and without the help I had every reason to expect from you."

The truth in that again touched Cayce, but uneasiness was changing to dismay. "Prices have been high. Orange crops have been good. What have you done with the money?"

For a long moment the judge looked at him, not smiling now. Instead of replying he said abruptly, "Surely you can stay for a few days. Only a few days. Then you can go back."

Astonishment tightened Cayce's nerves. Whatever he had expected the judge to say, it was not that.

"Why?"

Again the judge debated. Then he said, "Perhaps I need you."

"You've got Roddy."

"Still jealous of Roddy?"

"Is that all you want to say to me?"

For so swift a flash that Cayce could not be sure of it, there was a kind of flicker of uneasiness in the judge's face. He rose, as if aware of Cayce's scrutiny, pushing himself up with his hands spread out on the desk. The movement brought his face into green shadow.

The rain was slackening, the dull roll of a million tiny drums was passing eastward.

The judge said, "You're suspicious. You were always like that, Cayce. A difficult child. I thought perhaps these six years, your Army life, the job you managed to get, might have changed you. I'm only asking you to stay for—for a few days. It was merely a—a friendly impulse."

Cayce shook his head. "There's one thing I want to say. Then I'm going." The rain had diminished to a tinkling patter, so his voice rang out through the shadowed room. "You're doing a bad job with this place. If you've neglected the groves as you have the rest of the place . . ."

"Well," the judge said, "what would *you* do about it?"

And of course there was nothing he could do. He picked up his coat. The judge gave a little start, as if for the first time in all those years he'd questioned his power of command over Cayce. "There's nothing I can do," Cayce said. "But what are you doing with the money from the groves? Where is it going? Why haven't you spent any money on the place?"

"So . . ." the judge said, "so! Your father was right to leave things in my hands. You are unreasonable, impractical. You blame everybody but yourself. Your father knew you better even than I knew you or Blanche knew you then. It's just as well that he didn't live to see the kind of man his son has become."

"We'll leave my father out of this." He surprised himself by saying it quietly. All the frustrated and helpless furies of his boyhood seemed to gather together, reminding him of what he had so many times told himself he would do when he was a man, yet now he felt no anger.

The judge's fingers tapped the desk. "I see that my—my impulse, asking you to come, was a mistake."

For a second it seemed to Cayce that there was something very like sincerity in the judge's voice. He realized instantly that it couldn't be that. It was a trick of some kind, and just for a second it had almost deceived him. He said, quietly again, "I'll never come back while you are here."

Unexpectedly an almost hysterical rage flushed the judge's face. He seized the crystal orange and pounded it on the desk. "When I'm dead, you'll come back! You've said it in so many words—when I'm dead, you'll come back!"

"Yes," Cayce said. "When you're dead, I'll come back. But not until then."

He went out the door, and raindrops fell from the azaleas as he brushed past them. His feet splashed through the puddles along the path. Everything had gone wrong. He had determined to pin the judge down to some clear statement about the groves, the place, the judge's administration of it. Instead he had let the judge evade, answer indirectly, and take his old-time refuge in attacking him.

Cayce got into the car and backed around to enter the long lane between the Australian pines. But at the very end of the lane he stopped.

The road which led from the main country highway to his home on the east, and the Howard place on the west, came to a dead end there, against a barrier of great banks of hibiscus now in full and brilliant red bloom. Winding among the hibiscus there had been, long ago, a little path which ran along parallel to the boundary of his own groves down to another broader path which followed the curve of the lake to the old fishing pier. Nothing had been accomplished by his talk with the judge; he might as well have stayed in New York. But he could at least, by following that path, take a closer look at that portion of the groves.

He got out of the car, found his way to the gap in the hedge, and there was the old path half overgrown but still visible. The trees on his right stood in orderly ranks, their wet and glossy greens studded with bright orange fruit. But in

11

a matter of moments he knew that his anxiety was all too strongly justified. This grove, and certainly the rest of the two hundred-odd acres of groves, was in as bad and neglected a condition as the house. The house and grounds could be repaired. If the groves were let go too long, they were gone forever.

Suddenly he came out at the lake, flat and gray with the reflection of the gray sky. There was the path, overgrown with tough and springy crab grass, winding along between the groves on one side and the edge of the lake, grown over with rushes and reeds. There was the old fishing pier stretching out above the lake.

A girl was standing at the very end of the pier. She wore blue jeans and a white shirt and had a fishing rod in her hand. He thought it was Midge, and watched as she hooked in a fish. He was so near that he saw her give a little shudder before she braced herself and pulled the fish from the hook and flung it back in the lake. So it was a catfish she had pulled in, and he knew that it wasn't Midge, it was Dodie.

TWO

He looked at his watch and it was only a quarter after four. The talk with the judge had taken less time than he realized. He had all the time, and more, that he needed to get back to the airport. He walked slowly along the path toward the fishing pier. He could see the two boats tied at the east side of it, an outboard and a rowboat. So, thought Cayce, the judge still liked to go out onto the lake and fish. There was a mass of water hyacinth floating upon the surface of the lake. As he stepped on the pier and the weather-beaten boards rattled, Dodie turned.

She stared at him across the length of the pier. Her brown face and short, curly dark hair stood out against the gray of the lake. Her white shirt was open at the throat. Her blue jeans were washed and worn until they were almost white. Even at that distance it seemed to him he could see the deep blue of her eyes. Then she dropped the bait, hook, rod and all, and ran toward him. *"Cayce!"*

He was running too, and the pier shook and trembled. When he reached her he caught her tight in his arms. In a moment she pulled away from him and put her firm, brown hands on his shoulders, and looked at him.

She was beautiful, he thought, with a kind of shock. Little

12

Dodie, who had grown up in those six years. She said, "Why, what's the matter?"

"I guess I'm surprised. You're so pretty."

She laughed. "Why didn't you tell us you were coming?"

He didn't answer because he was still thunderstruck by her unexpected and vivid beauty. "I knew it was you," he said. "First I thought it was Midge, but then when you pulled the catfish off the hook I knew it was you. They always scared you. But you made yourself pull them off the hook."

"Cayce, have you come home to stay?"

"Well, no. I've got to go back to New York tonight."

"Tonight!"

"On the six o'clock plane. I came down this morning."

Her brown face, with its firm chin and broad forehead and straight dark eyebrows, was suddenly very sober. "Why?"

"The judge sent for me. Wrote me a letter. Said he wanted to talk to me. I thought I'd get it over with."

"Oh," Dodie said. Her hands dropped from his shoulders.

The lake had a turgid, almost imperceptible current which barely moved the carpet of entangled water hyacinth, so it looked as if it was slowly breathing. It had caught the fishing rod and Cayce saw its slow movement. "You're losing your rod," he said, and went to the end of the pier, boards rattling dully below his footsteps. He picked up the rod and put it down carefully, along the very edge of the pier, with the hook dangling over the water. Dodie followed him. "You taught me to put the rod there, so none of us would walk on the hooks—when I was about six." She gave a rather unsteady little laugh. "It's the first time I've forgotten."

And Cayce wished he could stay. From the end of the pier he could see the whole irregular sweep of the long lake. Its tiny inlets were hidden in reeds and brush, but he knew and had explored every one of them. His own grove cut off his view of the Howard place, Dodie's home. He turned to look up at his home. From one end of the pier he could see the house, and the distance, short though it was, softened the evidences of neglect; the gray wisps of Spanish moss hanging from the live oaks made a silvery curtain. Unconsciously his gaze lingered, fixing the house, the moment and place in his mind, as if he could take it away with him. The rain had left more vivid colors in its wake; the bougainvillaea bore deeper purple clusters. The azaleas were flame pink. Somewhere a jasmine was in bloom, for its sweet fragrance drifted to him above the muddy, fishy smell of the lake. All of it was home.

Dodie had been watching him. "You don't want to go back to New York."

13

"I hate it. I've always wanted to come home."

"You didn't tell us where you were," she said quietly. There was no reproach in it but there was a kind of sadness.

He looked away from the house into Dodie's eyes. "I couldn't," he said. "And then when I could, it was—I don't know—too late."

"That's not the only reason."

"I was so young, Dodie. It seemed to me that I had to make a clean break, put everything behind me, make some kind of life for myself, something that belonged to me. And then, sometime, I could come back."

"You mean when your uncle dies?"

Cayce replied as simply, "Yes. I can't live here while he's around, Dodie. And I can't get him out. There's just no other way for me."

"Oh, yes," Dodie said, "there's another way."

He knew what she meant. "No, that's out. There are too many of them. I can't fight them all. The judge, Aunt Blanche, Roddy."

Her blue eyes were so dark and so full of resolution that he looked away from her, for they attacked his own resolution. Down toward the east end of the lake he could see the roof of John Tyron's cottage; the rest of it was hidden by trees and shrubbery. One boat was tied up at the tiny platform which John used for a pier. Dodie turned away from him and went to the fishing rod. She touched it with the toe of her blue denim slipper, and said over her shoulder, "I always thought you left because of Midge and Roddy."

It was easy to cast his mind back to the years which had culminated in a boy of nineteen—Cayce Clary himself—leaving home with forty dollars in his pocket and something very like murder in his heart. Since his recent interview with the judge it was easy to comprehend the tide of emotion which had driven him away from home. He said slowly, "Perhaps it was partly that. Mainly, though, it was the situation at Blanchards."

"It's your home. It belongs to you."

"It was never home in that sense, after my father went away and died."

"It's home to you now." She turned to face him again. "You love it, Cayce. Don't go back to New York."

He tried to speak lightly. "If I don't turn up at the office tomorrow I'm likely not to have a job any longer."

Dodie came back to him and stood so close that he could see the small beat of a pulse in her temple. He had an odd impulse to touch her soft, brown cheek, put his hand on her

14

dark curls. She asked, "What did the judge want to see you about? Did he ask you to stay at home?"

"Yes. He didn't mean it."

Dodie was frowning, her blue eyes troubled. "Perhaps he did mean it, Cayce."

"The judge!" He laughed. "If he did mean it there was a reason, and a reason that would do me no good."

"You had a row with him."

"Yes. I suppose that's what it came to. I didn't intend to quarrel with him. I wasn't going to let myself care about anything he said. But of course it didn't work out that way."

"Cayce, Father says that you should have some kind of arrangement with the judge. Some legal and financial understanding."

"What?" Cayce said, and heard the bitterness in his own voice, and checked it. "Oh, what's the use, Dodie! He's got the place for as long as he lives. There's nothing I can do. . . ."

"Cayce!" someone called eagerly and excitedly from the path. Cayce whirled around. It was John Tyron running along the pier, both hands out. John was exactly as he remembered him, with his little, deeply lined and sun-tanned face, his small, gray, toothbrush mustache, his thinning, gray hair. He seized Cayce's hands eagerly. "Cayce! I knew it was you. I saw you both from my porch and I thought, it's Cayce. It can't be Cayce but it is!"

"I'm so glad to see you, John. I was afraid I wouldn't have time."

John's withered, usually rather sad and wistful face was beaming. "You've got to be a man. You're bigger."

Cayce laughed. "It's been six years."

John said, suddenly sober, "You're like your father."

Cayce's father had been not only John's closest friend but also, in a sense, his salvation. "He gave me something to live for," John had told Cayce once, "something to believe in." They all knew the story; John had joined the Army after his wife's tragic death in a car accident when John was driving. He had met Cayce's father and, two lonely, no longer young men, they had fought the war, and John's own personal problem of sorrow and regret, together. John frankly had hoped that he would not return from combat; but it was Cayce's father who was killed. But before he was killed he had talked John into coming to Val Roja when the war was over, and making a new life for himself. John had stayed in the Army as long as he could after the war; he had then come to Val Roja, as he and Cayce's father had planned. He

15

didn't perhaps succeed in making a new life for himself, as he might have done if Cayce's father had lived, but it was at least a different life, far away from his former home which, to John, had lost all purpose and meaning. And even as a boy Cayce had somehow understood that John transferred his almost mystic sense of gratitude—and dependence—from Cayce's father to Cayce himself. He ought to have written to John, Cayce thought guiltily.

John said suddenly, frowning, "What did you mean, saying you wouldn't have time? You're home to stay, aren't you?"

It was hard to tell John that he was leaving. Dodie guessed his reluctance. She said quickly, "Cayce says he must go back to New York on the six o'clock plane. I've been trying to get him to stay."

A lost, bewildered look came into John's face. "But Cayce —this is the place for you. It's your home. Don't go back to New York."

"No, I—I can't stay here." Cayce looked at his watch. "And I've got to get on my way right now if I'm going to make the plane. I'm sorry. I hate leaving right away, John. But I—I've got to."

He started for the path, avoiding John's troubled, lost-looking eyes, avoiding Dodie's resolute gaze. John and Dodie fell in beside him. The old pier rattled and wavered under their combined footsteps. Cayce automatically avoided a broken and unrepaired plank. John, trotting along, spoke jerkily. "Now Cayce—see here, if you don't want to stay in your own house, stay with me. Or at the Howards'. But stay. Just for a day or two."

Dodie said, "It's no use, John."

They brushed through the thick growth of hibiscus, which was still shedding raindrops, reached the car, and Cayce got into it. He leaned out and shook hands with John, who said, "It's the judge, of course. That's why you ran away. You ought to have come to me, Cayce. You ought to have talked to me before you left. You're like a son to me."

"Thanks, John. Take care of yourself." Cayce looked at Dodie. Her hand was on the car door, and her blue eyes seemed to have a message, strong and resolute, but nothing he could or would receive. He kissed her on the cheek this time, and in that fleeting instant he was aware of a sense of disappointment. Why hadn't he had the wit to kiss her red, lovely mouth, so generous and now very grave. Dodie said, "Cayce, don't go. Stay and fight it out with the judge."

He didn't dare wait and he didn't dare let them talk to him. His longing to stay would give his fancy a rosy color, suggest that he could successfully combat the judge. He said, "The judge and I can't live in the same house."

Dodie was still holding the door of the car. He kissed her squarely on the mouth. He thought that one of her hands went up to touch his cheek. Then he started the engine and the brisk thud was like the signal for the curtain to go down. This was home, this was his land. Here were Dodie and John, a loved part of his life. But in a moment it would all have vanished, the play would have finished.

Dodie said suddenly, above the thud of the engine, "Cayce, send me your address. There's something—there wasn't time —there's something I want to tell you."

At least that's what he thought she said; he nodded and waved, as the car shot away, leaving Dodie and John looking after him. When he reached the turn onto the main road he permitted himself to look back, but he was wrong. John was lighting a cigarette; Dodie had vanished.

He looked at his watch and it was past four-thirty; he speeded up. He'd barely make it to the airport. There might not even be time to drive into Tampa and leave the car at the garage where he had rented it. He'd have to telephone the garage from the airport and tell them to pick it up there. If he had stayed ten more minutes, five more minutes, he thought wryly, they'd have persuaded him, Dodie and John and even the house, where he knew a faintly rosy light would lie, for the cloudy gray sky was clearing and the sun was getting lower in the west.

He knew every aspect of the house as one knows every expression on a loved face. He knew it in the misty morning light and in the golden blaze of noon. But at sunset there was the most beautiful light of all, soft and misted, touching the house with rose and gold, gently sinking into a hazy blue.

In fact, he could not have expected the interview with the judge to be different in one word, one look, one thought from what it had proved to be. He had a strong sense of incompleteness about the whole interview, but that might have been expected too. The judge would never give up his hold on Blanchards.

He wished that he could have talked to Dodie for a longer time; that short interview was almost more tantalizingly incomplete than his talk with the judge. He'd asked nothing about Dodie, what she was doing, had she married and whom, although obviously she was living at home. Or perhaps not; perhaps she was married and only at home for a visit. He hadn't asked about her father, Henry Howard, and he loved Henry. He hadn't asked about Midge.

But Roddy was still living at Blanchards; he had gathered that from the judge's reference to him. Well, then, had he and Midge married? Where was Midge?

The traffic was heavier than he'd ever dreamed of encountering along that road. It was close to five o'clock; that accounted for it, of course. Again it struck him that the whole country had burst into activity and prosperity, for all those homecoming cars and trucks must indicate employment, new factories, new stores, a population increase which demanded them. He forced himself to be patient as the traffic was held up at a railway crossing for a long line of freight cars. On the outskirts of Tampa he saw the smoke from the factories rising against the rosy sunset. He knew by then that he couldn't get to the airport in time for the six o'clock plane.

He stopped at the first drug store he saw and telephoned to the airport; by luck there was a place on the nine o'clock plane; they would cancel his six o'clock reservation and hold a place for him on the later plane. He had some time to use up. He drove on into the city and slowly out along the Bayshore Drive and past the yacht club. He drove back and turned in the rented car. He took a taxi to the airport and then had dinner in the handsome, spacious dining room. The airport was new, huge, well planned, shining with efficiency and welcoming with comfort. He bought a newspaper and had a long drink, looking out the great window beside him onto the enormous field and watching the lights of planes as they arrived and departed. He finished dinner and as his plane was called went down to the main floor and out across the field, up the gangway and into the great, silver, shining bird which was to take him away from everything he loved and desired.

He selected a seat midway and unfolded the newspaper.

He was actually fastening his seat belt when he discovered that the battle was lost. He rose and walked out of the plane again, past the smiling stewardess who said something about the plane leaving in a moment. He replied absently and went back down the gangway. The lights were turned on now in the airport and shone ahead of him. His footsteps were hard on the pavement. The tropical evening air touched his face coolly. Behind him the plane was making a thunderous racket. He entered the building again and found a rack of telephone booths.

It took, as always, a long time to get the Val Roja line, for it was a busy one. When at last the operator said the line was free, he began to hope fervently that Dodie herself would answer, not Midge nor their father. It seemed right when Dodie's voice came over the wire, although it sounded very far away. "Dodie," he said, "you were right. I'm coming back."

"Cayce! Where are you?"

"At the airport in Tampa. I was on the plane but I got off. I can't help it. I'm going to stay and fight it out with the judge."

"Cayce, you can't come back! Get on the plane. Go back to New York. *Hurry!*"

Even the distance and the buzzing line could not account for the strangeness of Dodie's voice. *"Why?"*

"The judge was shot. They say it's murder."

He made some kind of sound.

"Nobody knows that you were here, Cayce. Nobody but me and John. If you stay, they'll say you did it. Get on the plane and don't tell anybody you were here."

He didn't really hear what she said, for a sense of paralyzing incredulity caught him. He didn't believe the judge was murdered. There was some mistake. The air in the booth was stiflingly hot.

Dodie's voice came again, thin and far away and unlike Dodie. "Send me your address. I'll tell you all about it and— I told you, there's something I didn't tell you this afternoon. I—but hurry, Cayce. Get on the plane."

There was a click in his ear and the line began to buzz sharply. He wasn't aware of putting down the telephone; he wasn't aware of walking out from the booth, coat over his arm, or looking out the broad glass windows toward the New York plane still standing there, about to leave. He turned and pushed through straggling groups of travelers to the main entrance. A rank of taxis stood there, yellow and white in the light. He opened the door of the first one, and a hand clamped down hard on his arm.

"Are you Cayce Clary?"

It was a state trooper. Another came briskly to his other side. "Yes," Cayce said.

They slapped his pockets matter-of-factly and bundled him into a police car, which was parked near the rank of taxis. He heard the announcement over the radio in the car: "Got the Clary fellow. Picked him up at the airport."

THREE

"What's this all about?" Cayce asked.

"Sheriff wants you."

"See here—I didn't kill the judge . . ."

19

"Save it."

They swerved around the airport and into the new highway, back toward Val Roja, and all Cayce's quarrels with the judge went with him like invisible baggage strapped to his back. His old enemy, his father's stepbrother, his uncle, the one-time judge, the man he'd seen and talked to and quarreled with—but for the last time—only a few hours ago, was now dead and he could not believe it.

After a while one of the troopers told him he could smoke if he wanted to. Later the other one asked him where the road to the lake turned off the main highway. Cayce told him, for of course he knew every inch of the winding country road they had turned into. It was dark by then but he knew just where the Howard fence began, he knew just where his own land began. Long strands of Spanish moss waved from the great water oaks at the edge of the road and reflected the lights from the car in silvery gleams. They reached the dead-end road, and lights from the Howard house sparkled through the intervening trees and shrubbery. "Turn right," Cayce said. They turned into the long, narrow tunnel between the great ranks of Australian pines and entered Blanchards, the Clary place, Cayce's own home, his own land, and now altogether his own.

But he wouldn't have wanted the judge to die like that.

There *must* be some mistake, he thought again. The judge always had guns around; where there are guns there are sometimes accidents. The police car shot out of the tunnel and into the circle at the side of the house. There were lights and men down near the lake and the old fishing pier, where he had had that brief talk with Dodie; the lights were west of it, though, and obscured by the grove. Was that where they had found the judge? The car stopped beside the long, white house. There were cars parked around the circle. One of the troopers took a hard grip on his arm and steered him along the path at the side of the house to the door of the study.

Again the study was lighted. There were three men inside it—among them John Tyron, who came quickly to meet him. "This is a devil of a thing, Cayce!" His wrinkled face looked ashy.

The trooper pushed Cayce into the room ahead of him. "Here he is, Sheriff. Got him at the airport."

A fat man, his face sun-wrinkled and brown, his eyes a bright hazel, said, "Hello, Cayce." It was Luke Weller, who had been sheriff of Suncas county, reëlected and reëlected ever since Cayce could remember.

The trooper said, "He was on the passenger list to New

York. The stewardess said he'd got off the plane. He was getting into a taxi when we picked him up. He already knew about the murder. Said he didn't kill the judge."

It was a completely detached and impersonal statement, neither for nor against Cayce, merely a fact. "That was a darn fool thing for me to say," Cayce thought, but in a remote way, because they could not seriously suspect him of murder.

The sheriff nodded. "Thanks. Might as well sit down, Cayce. We've got to have a talk."

"Luke, are you sure it wasn't an accident?"

The sheriff gave Cayce a queer long look. "It wasn't an accident."

The trooper vanished. The third man, who wore a sweat-stained leather belt and holster and must be the sheriff's assistant or deputy, followed the trooper.

"Can I stay, Luke?" John said.

"Sure," the sheriff said, "but I'll do the talking."

John hesitated then sat down very quietly, like an obedient child. The green-shaded light shone on his knobbly, bare brown knees, below gray shorts. His wrinkled face was in the shadow.

Cayce said, "Luke, what happened?"

"The judge was shot. You knew that, didn't you? You got off the plane."

"I got off the plane before I knew the judge was dead. When was he found? Where?"

"How did you know that the judge was killed?"

"I phoned to Dodie. She told me."

The sheriff knew Dodie; he knew everybody in the county; he nodded, hitched up a belt which precariously anchored wrinkled trousers, and moved to the desk chair. His tanned face glistened moistly; there were wet patches on his white shirt. A tray stood on the desk, holding a dented silver pitcher beaded with moisture and some glasses. The sheriff poured a glass full of water, drank it thirstily, and looked at Cayce. "Want a drink?"

Cayce gripped the slippery arms of his chair. "What happened?"

The sheriff set his glass down slowly. "Well, son, I guess first I want to know what's been happening to you. You haven't been home for quite some time. Six years, isn't it? Today the first time you got back since you ran away?"

"I didn't run away. That is, I suppose I did run away, but I was nineteen. Old enough to be on my own."

"Went to New York?"

21

"Not at first. Luke, this has nothing to do with the judge. . . ."

"Where did you go first?"

"Hitchhiked to Jacksonville. Got a job as a stevedore." The sheriff waited. "Then I got a job on a cargo boat going to New York. My stint in the Army was coming up, so I thought I might as well get it over."

"Did the judge know about that?"

"I suppose so. At least he knew my present address."

John said, "Why wouldn't he tell me . . ." and stopped as the sheriff shot him a silencing glance. The sheriff said, "Your father would have liked your being in the Army. What did you do when you got out?"

"I went to New York and got a job as a sort of adult errand boy in a brokerage firm. Went to school nights. Learned a little. Worked into selling . . ."

"Doing well, are you?"

"No. But I've got a job."

John lighted a cigarette; the match sputtered and its tiny flame revealed the tense, anxious lines in his face. Someone hurried along the hall outside the study; it sounded like a woman's feet tapping along the straw matting. Was it Blanche?

The sheriff said slowly, "I guess you liked being independent. You and the judge never got along."

Cayce didn't reply to that; there was no need. The woman's footsteps outside bothered him; he had no love for Blanche, but she was the judge's sister and his father had loved her. He said, "How is Blanche?"

"I think she's all right. It was a shock, of course. Old Dr. Hastings was here and saw her. Didn't you see Miss Blanche this afternoon when you were here?"

"No, I wasn't here long."

"Did you see Roddy?"

"No—how did you know that I was here, Luke?"

"Zack saw you."

Zack, of course; Zack was always somewhere about, invisible perhaps, but there.

John said suddenly, "I wouldn't have told them, Cayce. Dodie wouldn't have . . ."

A steely gleam in the sheriff's eyes sharpened. "So you and Dodie saw him. Well, we'll come to that later. Now then, Cayce, you're going to think this is your private business, but there's no such thing as anybody's private business when it's murder. Besides, I guess everybody around here knows

22

pretty well how things stood with you and the judge. How old were you when your father went off to war?"

"Nine. That was in nineteen-forty."

"There was some talk about it—oh, there's talk about everything around here. Some thought your father had no business going to war, since that was before we were in it and he was overage. But I don't know." The sheriff thought for a moment. "To tell you the truth, I sort of envied him. Did what he thought was right. It wasn't as if he hadn't had a brother and sister here to see to you and the place."

"Not really a brother," Cayce said tightly. "Not really a sister."

"Kin," the sheriff said temperately. "People he could trust to see to his boy if he was killed." A little flame of the old boyhood anger stirred in Cayce. The sheriff said disconcertingly, "Keep your head now, Cayce. Miss Blanche says your father didn't leave a will. Instead, he made out a deed to this place, a deed to you. Where is the deed?"

John burst out quickly, "You don't have to answer that, Cayce."

Again the sheriff checked him. "If you don't keep out of this, John, you'll have to leave."

"It's all right, John," Cayce said. "I don't know where the deed is, Luke. I don't think it was ever recorded. I expect it's over there." He nodded toward the battered old safe in the corner.

"You knew all about the deed?"

"Oh, yes. Everything was hurried there at the last. My father called me in here and sat over there at the desk and told me about it." He could see his father, brown and thin, but with a look of youth, drawing a nine-year-old boy to his knee and trying to explain so he would understand. "He said that he was giving me a deed to the place but that I was a minor, and somebody would have to see to me and the groves. He said Uncle Cayce would be here, and Aunt Blanche."

Cayce had always wished he had not been named for the judge, Cayce Moore, even as he had wished, when it struck his father that the Clary grove should have a name, he had not made it Blanchards, which was a contraction of Blanche and orchards. Actually, his father knew by then, as well as anyone, that they were never orchards, they were groves. But Cayce was Cayce and the place was Blanchards and it was an indelible mark upon them both. Cayce went on. "And then my father told me that he had written into the deed a life tenancy for the judge."

"You didn't know then just what that meant?"

"I knew later," Cayce said shortly.

The sheriff said thoughtfully, "Of course, if you and the judge had got along, it wouldn't have mattered. These have been prosperous years for Florida. This place ought to be able to support you and the judge and Miss Blanche—and Roddy too, for that matter. No trouble about that."

Surely the sheriff had seen the neglect the place had been permitted to fall into; he was too wise, too thoroughly experienced not to have seen that. "We would never have made a go of it, Luke," Cayce said. "Living in the same house, trying to run the groves together—I couldn't."

"You knew that that life tenancy meant that you couldn't get the judge out of here as long as he lived?"

John got up. "Look out, Luke! You can go too far!"

"I'm not making accusations. I'm asking legitimate questions. You can keep quiet or get out."

John hesitated and then sat down again. Cayce said, "I didn't kill the judge to get him out of here. You've got to tell me what happened."

Luke sighed and poured more ice water. "Start at the beginning, Cayce. Why did you come here today?"

"I got a letter from the judge. That was Saturday. It's the first time I had heard from him, or anybody here, since I left home. I didn't tell anybody where I was, so he must have got my address from the Army. He asked me to come here. He said he wanted to see me. That's all. He didn't say why. I wanted to talk to him, too. The banks were closed Saturday and Sunday. I got enough cash for the trip at the office early this morning, explained to my boss and came."

"Did the judge expect you today?"

"No. But I knew I could find him somewhere. I thought he'd be at home, and he was."

"Seems a long way to come without telling your uncle just when you'd be here," the sheriff said thoughtfully.

"Well, that's what I did," Cayce said shortly. "But I was going back again tonight. I took the morning plane down from New York and got to Tampa a little after one. I intended to make my talk with the judge just as short as possible. So I rented a car and drove around awhile and then I got out here just before four—about—twenty minutes to four, I think. If the judge hadn't been here I was going to look for him, but he was here. I asked him why he'd sent for me. I asked him what was happening to the place. There's neglect everywhere—you know that, Luke. He said that I had left just when I could have been of some use to him. I asked him what had happened to the money from the groves."

"Zack said you had a first-class row."

"So Zack was listening. I didn't see him."

"Go on, Cayce. You quarreled with the judge."

"Well, yes. The judge asked me to stay and I said I wouldn't. Finally the judge said he was here and would stay here as long as he lived, and I said . . ."

"You said that when he was dead you'd come back," the sheriff said.

John cried sharply, "Don't admit that, Cayce!"

This time the sheriff only eyed John soberly. "That's Zack's story."

"Where was Zack?" Cayce asked.

"He says he had started to the study here to talk to the judge and heard your voices. He ducked back into the shrubbery. Then you came out and he heard your car leave. . . . So you say the judge sent for you because he wanted to persuade you to stay at home?"

"He said only for a few days. He didn't, or he *wouldn't*, say why."

"Sounds as if you think he had some other reason for sending for you."

"I'm not sure. Somehow I just felt that there was something else—but he couldn't make up his mind to tell me. I came because I thought it was time I saw how the place was being run."

"Why did you change your mind and get off the plane?"

Cayce got up and poured some water into a glass. How could he explain it to anybody? "Because I—just couldn't go back to New York. This is my home. All at once I—got off the plane, that's all."

"Well," Luke said slowly, "maybe I can understand that. I'm not sure many people would. . . . I take it that you saw John and Dodie after you left the house?"

"She was at the fishing pier. John saw me and came to the pier too."

"I'd have thanked you if you'd told me that, John," the sheriff said with an edge in his voice.

John said nothing. The sheriff turned back to Cayce. "When did you start back to Tampa?"

"About four-thirty. The traffic was heavier than I expected. When I knew I was going to miss the six o'clock plane I stopped at a drug store and phoned and changed my reservation. Then I drove out along Bayshore Drive. I came back and turned in the car and took a taxi to the airport and had dinner there. And then—well, when I was on the plane and it was about ready to leave, that's when I decided to come back and stay here. I went to a phone booth and called the Howard's number. Dodie answered. I was going to ask her to put me up at the Howard place tonight, and then I'd see the judge in the morning. I didn't have any plan. I just knew I was going to stay. And then Dodie told me about the judge."

The sheriff said unexpectedly, "Dodie's the one you eloped with, isn't it?" There was a twinkle in his eyes.

"Why—yes." Cayce said, startled. Suddenly it seemed strange that when he talked with Dodie that afternoon he had never once thought of their childish and brief elopement.

John exclaimed, *"When was that?* I never knew about it!"

"I guess I'm the only one outside the family that did know it," Luke said. "Your uncle went hell-for-leather after you, didn't he?"

"Sure. Walked into the justice of the peace's parlor just as he'd married us. That was in Georgia."

"I remember." The sheriff eyed him thoughtfully. "What did you do that for, Cayce? I always thought it was the other girl, Midge, that you were sweet on."

Cayce thought back to that unreal day. If he told the truth, he would have to say he didn't know why he had persuaded Dodie to marry him and why she had consented. He said, "It was silly. Both of us were relieved when the judge had it annulled. He came walking in and made Dodie drive home with him and I drove my old car behind them. He took Dodie home and the next day said it was being annulled. A few weeks later—well, I guess it was a couple of weeks later that I left home."

"Well, that's in the past. It isn't the first time two kids eloped and maybe wished they hadn't. The judge did you a good turn that time, Cayce. You and Dodie Howard, too." The sheriff sighed. "I'm sorry you had that row with the judge this afternoon, Cayce."

"But look at the place, Luke! He was supposed to see to it. Where's the money gone!"

"Now, Cayce, you don't have to get mad. You're sure he wasn't sending you money?"

"Of course," Cayce said wearily. "I can prove it. Look at his canceled checks."

"You'd better tell me the name of the garage where you rented the car."

"It was Nathan's Garage. But I've got no alibi, if that's

26

what you want. . . . Luke, you've got to tell me about it."

John said, "You've got to tell him all about it, Luke. It's not fair to question him like this before he knows what happened."

"I'll do what I please," the sheriff said irritably but he looked troubled. "The fact is, Cayce, we don't know much about it. Not yet. There hasn't been time. All we know is that the judge was away from the house when Miss Blanche and Roddy got home; they'd been in Tampa. They think they got home about a quarter to six. Zack says he waited around to see the judge after you left but the judge didn't come out to the tool sheds as he usually does. The judge didn't come back into the house either, at his usual time, and Miss Blanche sent Roddy to look for him. His car was here so he hadn't left the place, and the boats were in so he wasn't fishing. Roddy didn't find him, so he came back. They weren't alarmed, no reason to be. And then . . ." He looked at John. "You can take it from there, John."

John's anxious, wrinkled face was still in the shadow but the light fell on his hands, which were lighting another cigarette with unsteady fingers. "I found him!" he said in a kind of burst. "I was fishing, down there beyond the pier. I saw something white and it looked like—well, I went to see and it was the judge. Dead. Shot. No gun. Nobody anywhere—on the lake or anywhere around. I came up to the house and told Roddy. Zack was here and we called him. We called the doctor and—and then Luke. Miss Blanche heard us." He got the light for his cigarette, which wavered in his lips, and took a long breath.

"Is that all you know?" Cayce said after a moment.

"That's all," the sheriff said. "We don't even know yet just when he was shot. It was about six-thirty when John found him. Have you got anything to add to this, Cayce?"

"No! Am I under arrest?"

"Why should you be under arrest?"

"Well, the way you questioned me . . ."

"Have to question. May have to question a lot of people. Yes," the sheriff said thoughtfully, "a lot of people. You wouldn't know this, maybe, Cayce, but a long time ago there was a rumor that the judge knew a few shady characters. That was in the days of rum-running. I can't say I know much about that myself, but they do say that along the Keys there was a flourishing traffic for a while. That of course was ended long ago. And, as I get it, the judge got respectable and was even appointed judge. He wasn't judge long, it was just to fill out somebody's term, but of course everybody still

27

called him judge. Guess we do that in the South; once a man's a judge we call him judge for the rest of his life. But while he was judge he handed out some pretty stiff sentences. And then he wasn't always easy with the men that worked here on the place. I don't know; I'm only a county sheriff. Looks like I've got a lot of work ahead of me." He got up slowly, pushing himself up wearily, with his hands on the arms of the chair. "Still, you'd be surprised how often these things do work out —usually pretty simple too. . . . You thinking about staying here?"

The question astonished Cayce because the answer was so obvious. "Yes."

The sheriff nodded slowly. "Guess you're right. It's your place now. Nobody to hinder you. Do anything you want to do."

"Luke, I didn't murder him. I hated him maybe, at least when I was a boy I hated him. But I didn't kill him."

"If I was you," the sheriff said, "I'd start with that west grove. Weeds everywhere. Needs disc-harrowing." His unwieldy body jerked around with surprising swiftness as footsteps pounded up along the path and the door flung open.

"Sheriff . . ." It was one of the state troopers. "We found some footprints."

Another man, a deputy, pushed the trooper aside. He was panting. "Luke, remember that guy that always went barefoot? Deeler—Barefoot Deeler they called him. He used to do odd jobs. Worked for a while up on the Howard place— oh, must have been twenty years ago. Well, he got let out of the penitentiary two days ago, it was all in the papers. There's footprints down there and whoever made them was barefoot. They're in that bit between the path and the grove. They're kind of blurry, but prints of bare feet."

The sheriff looked at the state trooper. "I guess we're going to want a little help from you boys. We haven't got much in the way of photography stuff and laboratories." He hitched up his belt and started out, the trooper and the deputy with him. Cayce caught at his arm. "Luke, who is this Barefoot Deeler?"

"Barefoot Deeler? The judge sentenced him to fifteen years. People didn't think it was right."

He went out and the screened door banged behind him. For an instant the men's crackling excitement almost drew Cayce along with them, in the contagious excitement of the hunt.

But this was a manhunt. It struck him coldly that he was on the wrong end of it. John said, "I'll go and see what's it's all about. Don't admit anything, Cayce." He put his hand for a second on Cayce's shoulder. Then he too ran out into the night.

FOUR

The small crystal orange with its delicate gold tracings and green-enameled leaves, which his father had designed and ordered as a token of the sale of his first orange crop, still stood on the desk where the judge had dropped it. It is tradition in that rich and lovely land: the grove owner marks his first sale with a gift to his wife. By then Cayce's mother was dead, but Lawrence Clary had followed custom nevertheless. Cayce picked up the orange and wiped it off carefully with his handkerchief, as if he could remove the traces of the judge's angry, grasping fingers, pounding the fragile crystal on the desk as if it were a hammer.

And now he had to see Blanche.

He went into the hall and along the straw matting to the wide, comfortable living room. There were long windows looking down upon the lake. The room was lighted, and in its old mahogany furniture, its faded chintz, was ineffably familiar to Cayce. So was the woman who stood at one of the windows peering down at the lights around the lake.

The tie between Cayce Clary and Judge Cayce Moore and Blanche Velidas (born Blanche Moore) was not a tie of blood—which had consoled Cayce many times during his boyhood. His father, however, had considered it a very close tie, perhaps because the three were brought up in the same household.

Lawrence Clary was a man of ideals, never quite practical, never quite hard enough and sensible enough, always observing only the best in other people, and Cayce loved him for it. After his father, in pursuance of those same ideals, had gone to war, he had been proud of him but many times had regretted it too.

His father had always, too, felt himself under a certain obligation to the judge, for when Lawrence Clary had bought the land and planted the groves and built himself a house, the judge had somehow—Cayce was never sure just how—made it all possible. He knew now that the judge must have either lent him money or signed notes for him to cover the purchase of the land. The house was barely built when Cayce's mother

29

died and after that perhaps his father lost his first love for the place, too; but he stuck with it for his son's sake.

Somehow—Cayce was not sure just how that happened either—the judge was all at once one of the household.

It seemed natural too—or else he was so lost in the mist of his childhood that he couldn't remember just how or when it happened—that Blanche, the judge's sister (divorced then from her husband), and her own son Roddy came there to live. Gradually they became a part of the household too. They needed a woman. He remembered his father telling Blanche that.

Blanche never made decisions; the judge did that. She didn't mete out rules or discipline or punishment. She was never an adept at the particular kind of biting, baiting sarcasm which came so readily to the judge's tongue. But in her silence she backed him up. To Cayce they were two of a kind; when he thought of one, he thought of the other. He had no love for Blanche and less for Roddy. It struck him suddenly that now he could get rid of both of them.

Blanche sensed his presence and turned. She was a slender woman with thick red hair and a white face in that land of sun-tanned skins. She had thick, dark eyelashes over eyes which were the changing, mysterious color of swamp water; Cayce remembered the very day when he discovered that. It was a hot still day when the fish wouldn't bite, and he and the old hunting dog had wandered into the swamp which was forbidden territory. . . . Blanche wore a thin, pink dress, ruffled and unbecoming, and vaguely old-fashioned. She looked at Cayce and after a moment put out her hand.

"I heard you were here."

Somehow he knew that she debated kissing him, and realistically decided against it. He was realistic too; he wouldn't say that he was sorry about the judge. He said, "Where is Roddy?"

"He went to see Henry Howard—oh, some time ago. He wanted to borrow another car. They organized a posse. I think he was going with them. I don't know what they can do—they can't really search the groves and the swamps. . . . Have you had dinner?"

"Yes. In Tampa."

She turned to look down at the lights near the lake. Cayce said, "I'd better go down there."

She nodded and he went out the front door. His own house; his own land with, now, no one to share it, no one to interfere, all his own. All the same, he wouldn't have wanted the judge to die like that.

30

As he started down the steps of the porch Roddy came up them, the narrow Spanish face that he had inherited from his Spanish father looming suddenly into the shaft of light from a living-room window. "Hello, Cayce," he said.

They shook hands briefly. Roddy was exactly as Cayce remembered him, tall, slim, dark, and somehow elegant.

"What are they doing down there?" Cayce nodded toward the lights near the lake.

"Right now they're looking for more footprints. By the way, Cayce, don't you have a scar on your foot?"

"*Scar!*"

"Sounds as if you'd forgotten all about it. It was on your right foot, wasn't it?"

"Why, yes. Of course! I guess I've still got it. Why?" Then he knew why and caught at Roddy's arm. "Do you mean that they have found a scar on those footprints?"

"Oh, no. I just happened to think of that scar of yours."

"But you must have seen something."

"Well, they're a queer kind of footprints. Look for yourself."

"See here, Roddy, I didn't murder the judge and if I had I wouldn't have been running around barefooted."

"I tell you I just happened to remember it when I looked at those footprints. I'm going in to see how Mother is coming along."

Cayce went down the steps, aware of Roddy's footsteps across the porch and a bang at the door.

Once away from the light which streamed from the windows it was very dark; there was no moon or stars showing and the clouds were so low and heavy he could almost touch them. The lush, thickly growing shrubs made deep blotches of darker shadows. But the scent of the jasmine here was strong and sweet; he paused involuntarily, for its remembered perfume was like a welcome. There was a little rustle near him and Dodie came out from the shadows of a great clump of bamboos. She was still wearing the blue jeans and white shirt open at her slender throat. The oval of her brown face was pale in the night. She put her hand on his arm. "I hoped you'd come out. Why didn't you leave?"

"It wouldn't have made any difference, Dodie. Zack told them I'd been here."

"Does the sheriff know that you had a quarrel with the judge?"

"Zack was hanging around and heard part of it. I told Luke the whole thing."

She caught her breath sharply in a way that wasn't like

31

Dodie, who wasn't afraid of anything, turned to look down toward the lake, whirled around again and put her face so close to him that her lips brushed his cheek. "Somebody's coming! Don't tell anybody about that scar on your right foot. Not anybody!" In a flash she was gone deep into the shadows again, and a state trooper, his flashlight jerking, was running up toward him. He turned the light full onto Cayce's face, said something about the telephone and ran on toward the house.

Cayce's heart was thumping uncomfortably. Roddy and now Dodie talking about a scar he'd acquired so long ago that he had all but forgotten he had it! He *had* forgotten it until Roddy mentioned it. Yet Roddy had said the footprints were not clear so why had Roddy remembered that scar? And what did Dodie know about them?

He'd better see what there was to see. He ran down toward the lake, the lights and the men there.

The judge's body had been taken away, long ago probably, and Cayce was relieved about that. There was a kind of depression in the reeds where the sheriff told him the judge had been found, close to the lake with only reeds and the thick carpet of water hyacinths intervening between it and the lake. It was, of course, close to the old fishing pier where he and Dodie had talked that afternoon.

The footprints which the men had discovered were not close to the judge's body but were found on the grove side of the path in the firmer soil; he looked at them and there were four to be seen in the slanting beams of the flashlight. They had been made by bare feet—there was no question of that— but they were blurred and broken; if a scar showed on one of them it was not visible to his eyes. The footprints lost themselves in the rough hummocky land of the grove and in the neglected undergrowth of weeds.

"Are there any more?" he asked the sheriff.

"We can tell more about it in the morning when it's light. There were none of them around the body and of course nothing would show in this path with all the crab grass covering it. We walked around some near the body but I didn't see any footprints there. There may be some more in that grove. These look kind of as if somebody had tried to destroy them, don't they?"

"Yes." That was exactly what they looked like; it was the only thing that could account for their uneven and broken outlines.

"I guess somebody could maybe stay on the path where

no footprints could show and reach out with a broken branch . . ." The sheriff eyed Cayce above the gleams of the flashlight and Cayce nodded. "Looks that way," he said.

"Well," the sheriff said, "we've done about all we can do tonight. The State Police will work on the footprints tomorrow. My guess is that they aren't clear enough to be very valuable, except they certainly do look as if they were made by bare feet. We've got road blocks all over the main highways. I don't think they'll pick up anybody. If it's Barefoot Deeler, he's lost himself somewhere. He knows the country."

One of the men (a deputy wearing civilian clothing) was putting white twine around stakes outlining footprints. The white twine looked clear and ghostly in the glancing rays of the flashlight.

And then for a long time it seemed to Cayce they stood around and talked. They were, of course, exploring possibilities, suggesting theories, but mainly, in excitement, talking it over. They always did that; it would be food for conversation for months. Roddy came back, his handsome face a guarded, listening mask. John, at Cayce's elbow, smoked feverishly and put in an occasional word.

Cayce listened to the cracker drawl, a little high-pitched, a little lazy, as natural to him as the fishy smell of the lake or the fragrance of jasmine. At last the sheriff clambered into a battered car which chugged into the black tunnel between the Australian pines and disappeared. The other cars followed, except for a police car which remained; for two troopers were to stay. "Keep your eyes open, boys," the sheriff had said to them before he left. That was, Cayce knew, so that no one could completely erase those footprints.

John said, "I'm glad you're home, Cayce, in spite of everything." He nodded at Roddy, then trudged off across the lawn to take the winding path through the east grove toward his cottage.

Roddy said, "Highball?"

"No thanks. I'm dog-tired."

They went up the wide old stairs, Roddy following Cayce and both of them instinctively quiet as they reached the upper hall. But there was no light showing beneath the door of Blanche's room.

Cayce's room was exactly as he had left it in the night six years ago. The bed was made up and turned down; Blanche had seen to that. He looked around the room feeling vaguely that something in it ought to stir him to sentiment. Nothing did; it was rather as if he had never been away, and every

33

book and every picture, even the worn spot on the rug beside the bed, was as familiar and accepted a part of life as if he had never left it.

When he got to bed he couldn't sleep though he really was as tired as a hunting dog. He wished he knew why Roddy—and then Dodie—had spoken of the scar on his foot. He turned on the light again, drew up his long leg and examined the thick white weal of the scar that ran diagonally across the ball of his right foot. It was still there, all right, it had been deep. But he had, in actual fact, all but forgotten it. He had got it in the lake, wading, on the jagged cutting edge of a broken bottle. Dodie had run to the Howard house for the antiseptic which old Judith always kept on the pantry shelf. Cayce could still see her flying figure and kind of blue overall arrangement with straps over her thin childish brown shoulders and her wiry curly pigtails flying. She had brought back bandages too and the cut had healed up and by unspoken consent nobody mentioned it to elders; already there were too many rules about playing in and out of the lake so they never told anybody about mishaps—not even the day when the alligator they called Old Stinker went on a rampage and butted against the pier and missed Dodie's dangling leg by a hair's-breadth. Cayce grinned a little at that memory and turned off the light.

There were small night sounds, distant and remarkably clear because the night itself was so still: a twitter of a bird, a slight rustling in the bougainvillaea outside the window. Once he heard the distant, coughing rumble of Old Stinker; Old Stinker was an alligator who had dwelt, for the most part, with extraordinary lethargy in the lake ever since Cayce could remember. The harsh rumble came again. If it wasn't Old Stinker, it was another one.

The police were going to examine the bullet that killed the judge—one slug, he gathered from their talk, which went through his heart. But they would never find the gun. It was in the lake, sinking more inextricably into its muddy bottom every moment. They had all agreed to that—Cayce, too.

In the morning he'd try to pin Roddy down to some sort of explanation for that question about the scar on his foot. And he'd talk to Dodie, too.

He wondered if Midge was at home and if he'd see her, and suddenly he wondered if Midge's smile still had the power to turn his heart over. It struck him as odd that he still hadn't asked anyone directly about Midge. Yet obviously she and Roddy hadn't married. Oh, well, she'd be married to somebody by now.

Wasn't it Midge he was sweet on, the sheriff had said. Everybody knew that. He had romped and played and fished and run races with Dodie; he had teased her and been teased back but he had never teased Midge. She was too precious, too lovely, too—no, he'd never romped with her, he'd only worshipped her. So when Midge and Roddy suddenly developed a young romance and said that as soon as they were of age and their families would permit it they were going to be married, Cayce and Dodie had eloped. Why? Cayce thought drowsily.

He had been hurt as only a boy who feels himself alone can be hurt, first by his father's death, constantly and helplessly by the judge, and then by Midge's engagement to Roddy. Had he then reached out for someone who would belong to him alone, Dodie? He couldn't now recapture any of the defiant impulse that had led to that elopement, with the judge following hotly at their heels and immediately annulling the marriage.

Well, Dodie was well out of that. Clearly from her frank and direct attitude that afternoon she had relegated it to its proper and unimportant place. Certainly it had never been really a marriage.

It struck him as strange that he knew so little of what had happened to Dodie or Midge or any of them during the past six years. Yet that had been his own doing; he had resolutely cut himself off from home and everything that meant home to him; it had seemed then the only way in which he could save himself. He took a long breath of the flower-scented humid air and went to sleep.

He did not know how much later it was when something roused him from that heavy sleep; he did not know either what it was that roused him, but he sat up abruptly, bewildered at first and then remembering in a flood where he was and what had happened. He was puzzled, too, to find himself listening with every nerve in his body.

It was very dark. It must be still cloudy and overcast. He then heard a slight sharp creak, which he knew as he knew the rest of the house. It was the third step on the stairs.

So that was all; Blanche was restless, wandering around the house, going down to the pantry to heat some milk as she often used to do. But he waited a while just the same. He had finished a cigarette when he heard the creak again and light footsteps, as if Blanche had tiptoed along in bedroom slippers past his door. Another door somewhere down the hall closed. He put out his cigarette. Again on the very edge of sleep he thought of the next day. The first thing he would do was take

35

a look at the groves and try to start what he knew would be a patient and laborious process.

What he actually did the next morning was fire Zack.

FIVE

Cayce got up late, not early as he had intended. A grove owner rises with the dawn. It was a cloudy still morning with mists hanging closely around shrubbery and trees, and the lake gray as the sky. If the troopers were still on the pier, he could not see them. He found some faded dungarees, too tight for him now but wearable, and a shirt which strained over his back muscles. A new maid was in the dining room, a neat pleasant Negro girl who told him that Miss Blanche was having her breakfast upstairs and Mr. Roddy had been up early and gone out and the grits were still hot. He hadn't had grits for breakfast since he left home; he ate two great helpings, drank thick black coffee, went out to find Zack and found him, regrettably, leaning against a tractor and conversing lazily with a couple of grove laborers. Nine o'clock, Cayce thought, and none of them at work.

Zack did not remove the cigarette which drooped from his loose mouth. His small cap with its enormous bill, intended to shield his eyes from the sun, was set low over his forehead. He didn't move a muscle of his slack body except to say, "Hello, Cayce."

The two workmen stared at Cayce. There was an easy insolence in Zack's greeting and instantly Cayce understood the big man's intention to exact every ounce of value from his position, which was a strong one. The judge was dead, and while he was alive (and while Cayce's father had been alive) it had been Zack in fact who ran the groves. Now that the judge was dead and Cayce might be expected to take over, Zack's position was even stronger. Cayce was inexperienced, he knew only what he had observed as a boy about the management of the groves and it had been Zack's knowledge that he had observed. So Zack was in the saddle and intended to ride high. Cayce said, "Why aren't these men at work?"

Zack shifted one thick leg. "Well, now," he drawled, his little eyes already gleaming with triumph. "I guess you and me have got some things to talk about, Cayce."

"That's right, Zack. What's been going on here? Why has the place run down like this?"

A dangerous flash came into Zack's eyes. "I've seen to this

36

place since before you were born. Nobody's complained yet."

"I'm complaining now." Cayce was aware of the gluttonous, avid attention of the two workmen; the story of the incident would be over Suncas County by nightfall. He knew that he stood or fell as a grove owner within the next five minutes.

Zack said, "If you don't like the way I run the place you know what you can do about it."

"The place is mine, Zack. You can work for me and take orders from me or . . ."

"Or what?" Zack gave an amused smile at the two laborers.

"Or get out," Cayce said.

In a way it was unfortunate that the two workmen were present, their eyes and ears strained with alert curiosity, for Zack knew too that his position rose or fell in that moment and for over twenty-five years as superintendent of Blanchards he had been a man of some power in the community. A rattlesnake gleam came into his eyes. He straightened slowly and stood facing Cayce, a big shambling figure of a man but powerful too. He dropped his cigarette without crushing it, which annoyed Cayce; it was a small thing yet typical of the neglect and shoddiness the place had fallen into.

"Okay," Zack said, "if that's the way you feel about it I guess I'll get out."

He sauntered over to a car which stood in the drive. He wore, as always, khaki-colored slacks and shirt; it was like a uniform which marked him as a cut higher than a mere workman; even from the back he looked insolent and certain of his own power. He got in the car, drove around the house and vanished behind the Australian pines. The two workmen stared spellbound after him.

So he was gone without telling Cayce anything about what had been done, what had not been done, and what work should be laid out. Where were the supplies? What was the condition of the machinery? Fertilizer was needed; the groves had to be sprayed. For a second Cayce resisted an impulse to call him back; that wouldn't do. He turned to the workmen.

It was close to noon by the time he had sent the big tractor into Val Roja for repairs, started the other man clearing the west grove with the small tractor and made a tour of machine and supply sheds where he found just about what he had expected: neglect, rusted and unrepaired machinery, careless and costly disorder everywhere.

He went from the shed to the plot for new trees, young trees designed to replace the older trees as they died or dwindled. The young trees were mere twigs, obviously untended.

And there was so much to do. The place was large enough to keep five men busy. He'd get two more men and act as superintendent himself; gradually he might be able to bring order out of the chaos.

There must be records, of course. He'd take a look at the groves' books and receipts. He scooped up a handful of the rich brown soil, good hummock land. All it needed was care. As he crumbled it through his fingers, rejoicing in the touch of it, he could see the place as he would make it: acres of fine clean groves, the trees laden with fruit. He was so lost in his dream that he did not see Roddy until he spoke. "I hear you fired Zack," Roddy said.

Cayce looked up with a start. Roddy was standing, watching him, a picture of the gentleman of leisure in his well-tailored brown shorts and white shirt.

"Who told you that?"

"As a matter of fact I met him down near the gate. Aren't you getting a little ahead of yourself? You can't replace Zack. He's been on this place forever."

Cayce was grubby, hot and uncomfortable in the clothes that were too small for him. He eyed his cousin's leisurely elegance. "What's wrong with you taking a hand?"

Roddy's narrow face sharpened. "I have other things to do."

"You still live here, don't you?"

"Of course!" Roddy eyed him for a second. "Oh, I see. You've still got Midge on your mind. Is it possible that nobody told you?"

"Told me what?"

Roddy laughed. "You ran away because Midge and I were engaged. Is that why you stayed away all this time? What a joke on you!"

"I suppose you mean that you and Midge never married. Why not?"

Roddy shrugged. "We were too young, for one thing."

"Where is Midge?"

Roddy's black eyebrows arched themselves in ostentatious surprise. "Why, I thought you'd know! She's at home, of course. Do you mean you haven't seen her? She's lovely, Cayce, well worth seeing."

His silky tone reminded Cayce of the judge. Cayce said abruptly, "Have you been helping the judge with the groves? There are some things I want to know."

Roddy's eyebrows came down straight above his thin Spanish nose. "No," he said shortly, "I have nothing to do with

38

the groves. I've got a job and a good one. With the Velidas Cigar Company."

Cayce remembered dimly that Roddy's father, Blanche's long-divorced husband, had been some sort of cousin to the Velidas family, which in the main owned and operated the rich Velidas Cigar Company. "That's fine," he said heartily. "I expect you'll want to go to live in Tampa now that the judge is dead. And take Aunt Blanche with you."

There was a deep flash in Roddy's eyes. "You do want to get rid of us, don't you? Somehow I don't think it's that simple."

And what exactly is behind that? Cayce thought. For an instant it was as if the judge had spoken, certain of himself and his power, silky, taunting and arrogant until Cayce rose to the bait.

Except now he didn't. Why, he thought with amazement, that's gone! *Nothing Roddy can say, nothing Blanche can say, nothing they can do can touch me.*

In a great rush of freedom, of having escaped those invisible shackles of his youth, he smiled at Roddy. "Take your time," he said. He wanted to go to the Howard place. He started for the great lines of Australian pines which loomed into the pearly gray sky.

His good humor baffled Roddy. He frowned and then followed Cayce. "The sheriff phoned. He's coming out this morning."

Because the judge had been murdered. For an instant that seemed an extraneous event, removed from Cayce, nothing to do with the first and primarily important thing in his life, Blanchards.

He looked at Roddy. "Why did you ask me about the scar on my foot, Roddy?"

His direct attack seemed to startle Roddy, who was a born intriguer, indirect by nature. His reply, however, was prompt. "Because of the footprints, of course. They weren't clear. They looked as if somebody had purposely tried to destroy them. Naturally that would be because there was something identifiable about the footprints. I don't know much about police work but I should think it would be very hard to identify just a bare footprint; maybe I'm wrong. But I—well, I just thought of your scar, that's all. By that time, of course, I knew you had seen the judge." It was glib and prompt—too glib and too prompt.

"So you leaped to the conclusion that I must have shot the judge?"

39

"I thought it very likely you'd quarreled."

"And I crept up on bare feet to take a shot at him? Why? Oh, I see. To suggest it was this Barefoot Deeler." His new-found assurance still operated. He eyed Roddy with curiosity. "I suppose that's what you'd have done. I'm not that clever. I remembered Barefoot Deeler vaguely when they talked of him, but that's all. What do you know about him?"

"It was all in the newspapers the other day. It seems he was up for manslaughter; he'd had a fight with a man in a bar. The man died of a concussion. There was a question as to whether Deeler hit him or whether he stumbled and hit his head on an iron table. The jury had to find Deeler guilty but recommended a light sentence, something like that. Instead the judge gave him fifteen years."

"Who was the man that died?"

"A young fellow from a Cuban family in Ybor City." He pronounced it, as all Tampans do, Eboe City. "There are a lot of votes in Ybor City. Some people said that the judge had an idea he might want votes sometime. But I wouldn't know."

They had reached the circle beside the house and the sheriff's car wasn't there. "I'll go on over to the Howards'," Cayce said. "Phone me when the sheriff gets here."

He strolled off along the driveway, aware of Roddy's still regard following him until the Australian pines came between them.

It was cooler there, although the towering harsh branches of the pines almost shut out the gray sky. The carpet of brown pine needles was slippery under his feet. In the west grove, parallel to the driveway, and between it and the lake, he could hear the small tractor humping along over the ruts. He must get his mind off the grove and onto murder. He was their main suspect if this man they called Barefoot Deeler proved to have nothing to do with it. Fifteen years was a long time to hate a man; murder after you had just emerged from prison was a long chance to take. Deeler would have known that the police would pick him up at once. But if Barefoot Deeler hadn't shot the judge, then who had killed him?

The judge had made enemies certainly, but murder—that's different, Cayce thought. There's got to be a reason for it, something urgent, something terribly important to somebody.

A faint little chill crinkled his spine. He had a motive and a strong one.

And Cayce himself had now made an enemy of Zack.

Neither John nor Dodie would have admitted Cayce's presence or the knowledge of his quarrel with the judge, but Zack had heard something that sounded very much, too much, like a threat. "When you're dead, I'll come back." Cayce thought irresistibly of what a prosecuting attorney could make of those words. Zack would be the strongest witness for the prosecution, and how gladly he would relate that story in the witness box.

The only thing Cayce could do was to put his faith in the police and the truth. But he must find out exactly what Dodie knew of those footprints.

It struck him then that in a few moments he would see Midge. He couldn't imagine Midge having changed; he'd carried the small lovely image of her face along with him all those years and Midge was still free to love and be loved— at least certainly she had not married Roddy. His pulses didn't exactly quicken—he was too hot and had too many things on his mind—but he did rather wish he was wearing other clothes.

He came out from the Australian pines and crossed the road and there was the Howard place, the place of his dreams; in fact, the place he wanted Blanchards to become. The high metal fence was in perfect order, no sagging here, no fence posts down, and all the posts were concrete to foil the termites. No brush grew ferociously along the fence either; it was all as clean as the groves beyond it.

There were the great metal gates, fastened neatly back. The driveway itself was new since he left home; formerly it had been sand, packed hard and trim. Now it was a narrow, concrete ribbon with the edges clean and grassy. Lamps on high standards, like miniature street lamps, stood at regular intervals on either side. On his left the groves began and they were beautiful, green and luxurious; obviously they had been watered and fertilized and kept clean of brush.

The trees were laden with fruit. It would be an enormous crop. The oranges and grapefruit were now nearly ripe so it would soon be time for the pickers. As he neared the house, he passed great clumps of calamondins laden too, with what looked like tiny orange lanterns; there were kumquats, loquats and, Cayce knew, a large plot of Ponderosa lemons. Henry Howard, with his passion for experiment and his love for the land which bore so richly, had experimented with almost every kind of fruit-bearing tree. Cayce made mental notes about his own grove; he would ask Henry's advice.

Henry had always been kind to him; he was a scholarly man too and had taken pleasure and pains in somewhat informing Cayce's young mind. Cayce owed what knowledge of the classics he had, as well as an awakened curiosity and love for reading, to Henry Howard. He thought of the long afternoons on the terrace of the house ahead of him, with the heavy bougainvillaea and wisteria in bloom, as Henry read or talked or answered Cayce's questions in a way that a boy would understand. But Henry was also a practical administrator who understood groves.

Cayce came out of the driveway. An enormous oval swimming pool stood now close to the lake; it was banked up and bordered with pink azaleas in full bloom. A cabaña stood beside the swimming pool. Everything showed white and clean; only then Cayce fully realized how shabby the house at Blanchards had become, how desperately it and all the buildings needed repair and paint. But obviously the Howard place had flourished; Henry had no other income save that from his grove; clearly, then, the years had been good years for crops.

And then he saw Midge. There was no mistaking that slim graceful figure in a thin white dress. She was cutting camellias, carefully placing each bloom on a basket. He felt that his heart ought to pound, or something, but instead a verse flicked absurdly out of his memory, something Henry had read to him or made him read: "Charlotte, having seen his body borne before her on a shutter, like a well-conducted person went on cutting bread and butter."

He was instantly ashamed. What had murder to do with a girl like Midge? Besides she had always been self-controlled, tidy in her emotions; it was one of the things he had admired in her because his own emotions had been troublesome and turbulent, easily played upon by the judge. He forgot his too tight, now dusty and grubby clothes and ran across the thick green turf.

He had reached the great oval of camellias before she saw him. Her eyes widened—blue eyes, like Dodie's and still unlike Dodie's, for they were the light, placid blue of a kitten's eyes, while Dodie's were dark and sometimes very serious.

Typically she put down her scissors and a pink camellia before she said, "Cayce," and put out her arms. Her lips were soft and cool and fragrant as a rose. "Cayce," she said again and drew back in his arms to look up into his face. She was a tiny thing, exquisitely small; her face, in that sun-drenched land, was as pink and white as the camellias. "I hoped you would come this morning. Cayce, why did you run away? Why did you leave me like that?"

He replied literally, "Because you were engaged to Roddy."

"Oh, that." Midge gave a tiny musical laugh. "That was only a childish thing. It didn't last. It was you really all the time. Oh, Cayce, I so hoped you would come back some time and now you're here." She moved her face up toward him and he kissed her again and looked up as if a string had jerked him. Dodie stood now at the other side of the camellias. That day she was wearing tailored green shorts and a primrose yellow shirt, open at her slender brown throat. Her dark head was bare, showing its crisp dark curls, her blue eyes were very steady. Her mouth was steady too and rather firm. "Good morning, Cayce," she said.

SIX

With a pretty air of confusion Midge moved out of his arms. Cayce was scarcely aware of her movement, for there was something very serious in Dodie's gaze. He said, "Is there any news?"

Dodie shook her head. "No, But Father wants to see you. He's on the terrace."

Midge picked up her hat and set it carefully on her head. It framed her lovely face in lacy white; she picked up the basket of pink and white camellias and looked like one of them in her trim, yet graceful elegance.

Dodie said to Cayce, "Try not to notice the change in Father. He's almost crippled with arthritis."

"Henry! You didn't tell me yesterday."

"There wasn't time," Dodie said. "John Tyron is here, too."

Midge set her little chin. "And drinking! This early in the day."

Dodie said with a level look, "I offered him a drink. I knew he wanted it."

"I don't see why you encourage his drinking," Midge said.

"I don't encourage it. There are times when John just has to drink. If he's upset or thinking about his wife or . . ."

"Then he's upset too much of the time," Midge snapped. She turned to Cayce, "It's got worse since you left town. Dodie makes excuses for him but I don't think there is any excuse."

Dodie said quietly, "John blames himself. He was driving when his wife was killed. That makes it different."

A little pink came up into Midge's cheeks. "You always take his part, Dodie. And you like him too, Cayce, just because he was in the war with your father. He hasn't done another thing since he came here after the war and built that shack . . ."

"It's a nice little cottage," Dodie said.

Midge went on, ". . . On that strip of marshland your fa-

43

ther told the judge to let him have. He just fishes and potters around and drinks."

Dodie looked at Cayce. "He still keeps up the law practice he started in Tampa. At least he's got an office and—I guess it isn't much of a practice but he gets along all right. I was thinking, Cayce—maybe you need a lawyer."

Midge's light blue eyes widened again. "You don't mean—why you can't mean—on account of the judge!"

Dodie said steadily, "Father thinks so, too."

Midge cried, "But that's silly. Everybody knows this horrible man, the one they call Barefoot Deeler—he shot the judge. Cayce didn't shoot him."

Cayce said slowly, "Maybe I do need a lawyer."

"It wouldn't hurt," Dodie said. "If John doesn't think he can help you he'll suggest somebody who can, some other lawyer."

A spark of anger flashed in Midge's pretty eyes. "I think John's a lazy drunken coward. I know he was a good friend of Cayce's father but . . ."

"And a good friend of mine, too, Midge," Cayce said. . . . "Let's go to the terrace."

He slipped his arm around Midge's waist. He tried to take Dodie's arm, too, but she moved a little away from him so the three of them walked across the green slope, up toward the terrace, without speaking. The little sparks of conflict between Dodie and Midge ought to have taken all three of them back to their childhood but somehow this time it was different.

Looking up at the house Cayce felt a welcome pang of familiarity. It was a beautiful house, long and well proportioned, with architecturally perfect lines which made it seem to grow out of the soil, indigenous to the land. Even the shrubbery looked as if it sprang of its own will out of the soil. The bougainvillaea which framed the terrace looked as if it had chosen to make its home there. Some great water oaks, so enormous with their great trunks and spreading green foliage that nobody knew how old they were, looked as if they were an indissoluble part of the land. Royal palms, which Henry had put in long ago, stood with stately grace among them. Blanchards would be beautiful, too—when Cayce had had time to restore its beauty and to go on with his father's plans.

John and Henry were sitting on the terrace watching them. John raised one hand in greeting. Henry smiled. When they reached the bright stretch of the terrace Cayce saw the ramp built along one side of the steps and glanced quickly at Dodie.

"For Father's chair," she said in a low voice.

They walked up the steps and Henry sat very erect in a wheel chair and put out his left hand. "Cayce, my boy, welcome home."

It was lucky that Dodie had warned him; Cayce tried to conceal his shock at the sight of Henry Howard. He had been a big man, muscular, delighting in exercise. He was now shrunken and so thin his flesh seemed stretched over his big bones. His hair was white and his face was deeply lined. But his eyes were brilliant with welcome. "I was really afraid I'd never see you again."

Dodie said quickly, "Now you're better, Father. A month ago you couldn't move your right hand at all. Now you can manage your chair. Why, you ought to see him, Cayce! He zips around in that chair all over the place, sees to everything."

Cayce had never seen a wheel chair like the one in which Henry was sitting; it was big and padded and equipped with a small motor.

John said, "That's right. I saw you sailing along the driveway as if you were on a motorcycle. . . . How's everything, Cayce?"

"If there is any news I haven't heard it. Look here, John, you're a lawyer. Maybe I need a lawyer. How about it?"

John's withered brown face brightened for a second as if a flash of sunlight had crossed it. "I'd do anything in the world to help you, Cayce. If they don't find this Barefoot Deeler—or if they do find him and he proves he had nothing to do with the judge's murder, you'll be in a spot. You may need a better lawyer than I am—a good criminal lawyer."

There was a silence among them. Somewhere among the water oaks a bird sang softly. John looked at Cayce and then out across the lake and said, "You see, Cayce, I'm a little out of practice. Oh, I can draw a will or do odd chores but I don't do anything much in the way of—well, of anything important. What I'm trying to say is," he said with a kind of embarrassment, "I'll do anything to help you, but you know that."

Cayce said, "You're good enough for me, John."

Again the flash of brightness crossed John's face.

"But if it should come to a trial—I'm not saying it will, but if it should . . ."

"Then you can find me the best criminal lawyer there is," Cayce said.

45

Henry nodded. "Right now, John, tell us what you think of the situation."

John thought for a moment. "Well, of course, if they make a murder charge and I'm only saying if, they'll base it largely on motive."

Midge settled herself in the shade of a giant oak; her face looked even lovelier against the background of thick green shrubbery that edged the terrace; it cast faint green and gold shadows on her white dress. She wore thin stockings and high-heeled white pumps. Cayce's glance strayed to Dodie's slender bare brown legs as she moved to a chair. Midge, of course, would never go barelegged like that; even as a child she had dressed in frilly feminine clothes which never seemed to get dirty.

Henry said, "They can't convict a man on motive."

"No," John said, "but the establishment of motive carries weight with a jury. Cayce, have you ever talked to a lawyer about the judge's life tenancy at Blanchards?"

"No. No, I haven't."

"Why on earth not?" Midge asked sharply.

"I don't know," Cayce said slowly. "That is, I guess I do know. My father left things that way and he had reasons that seemed good to him. I wasn't going to quarrel with that. Besides I don't think family disagreements can ever really be settled by lawyers."

John said, "Nobody wants to go to law to try to settle family disputes. Besides you might not have got very far. A deed with a life tenancy written into it is exactly that. The deed is yours but the judge—had control of the place. As I understand it, he could have lived there all his life if he wanted to. A life tenancy is hard to define; it is not a usual provision for that very reason. Who's going to be able to say where the judge's interest should come under supervision in order to protect your interest? Your father told me about it; he expected things to be different. He felt the judge and Blanche would take care of you and the place, and a life tenancy for the judge would compensate him. Besides, it would automatically ensure his interest in seeing to the place. That was your father's view. He had complete confidence in the judge."

John looked out across the gray lake and said in a low voice, "We talked over everything, I guess. Joined up at the same time, got behind desks because of our age. Teamed up and got transferred to an active branch of the same outfit, got into combat the week after the D-Day landing." He broke off. "But you know all that."

Henry said, "John tells me you left here about four-thirty. Isn't there some way you can establish an alibi?"

"I don't think so. I went back to Tampa and drove around . . ." They listened while he repeated every detail.

Across the gray lake he could see moving black dots which were the Black Angus herd on the lush green slopes of the Burke place. Trees over there were laden with long wisps of Spanish moss, ghostly and gray. There was no Spanish moss on the giant oaks around the terrace; even as he talked, that other person in Cayce, the grove owner, thought that he must get some men in to get rid of the moss on his own trees and then have them sprayed so it wouldn't return. Many people said it didn't matter, it wouldn't hurt the trees but Cayce hated it; it was a parasite; once removed the trees became shapely, filled in with great spreading tents of gray-green foliage.

When he had finished John said, "The phone call for a reservation might help if they knew exactly when the judge was shot and I've got a notion about that. It was after six, close to six-thirty when I found him and . . ."

Henry interrupted. "How long do you think the judge had been dead when you found him?"

"I don't know. Dr. Hastings couldn't say either." John looked at Cayce. "He's the coroner now. He didn't get here for another hour. He said the judge had been dead by then probably a couple of hours but he couldn't be definite. When I called the sheriff, he told me to call the coroner and take over till Luke got here. You know, I'm a deputy sheriff."

It was the custom in that intensely circumscribed section of Suncas County. Suncas was a large county and the sheriff was short-handed. Outside the magic green acres of lake and grove land and meadow were the busy packed little towns, the phosphate plants, the big commercial packing, freezing and canning plants, the smaller cultivated plots for truck gardens, watermelons, strawberries. But there around Clary Lake dwelt the old-timers and from among them always Sheriff Luke Weller chose one or two deputies. Their duties were, as a rule, very light; rarely a prowler might be reported; once in a great while someone suspected a still. Henry had been deputy sheriff for many years and so had the judge.

"So," John went on, "I began to wonder about the time when the judge was shot. It's so quiet on the lake. It looks as if I'd have heard the gunshot and I didn't. But I do know there was a flight of heavy bombers going back to MacDill Field. They passed over the lake fairly low. If the judge were

47

shot just then I wouldn't have heard it. I asked Blanche; she said that she and Roddy were almost at the Val Roja Road when the bombers went over. Zack said he was out somewhere in the back working on a tractor. He told the sheriff he hadn't heard anything but the bombers. If the judge was shot when the bombers went over, Cayce was getting close to Tampa."

Henry said, "None of us heard anything. I was listening to the news. I think the girls were upstairs. You've got something there, John."

Midge said, "I heard the bombers. I didn't hear any shot. Dodie had her radio going, I could hear that."

"Morning, folks," said a voice from the lawn and beyond the thick lugustrums bordering the balustrade the sheriff's head bobbed into sight. Roddy strolled beside him up the steps.

"Hot," Luke said, collapsing in a chair at Henry's invitation and adjusting his belt over his large middle. He cast an eye on the sky. "It don't look like rain."

Roddy said to Henry, "Good morning, sir," nodded at John, smiled at the girls and went to sit on the balustrade near Midge.

Henry said, "You look as if you could do with a cool drink, Luke. What'll it be?"

It was like Henry; a graceful welcome to his house came first, even when his visitor was the county sheriff coming to investigate murder.

Luke fanned his face with his hat and glanced at John's empty glass. "They say a policeman shouldn't drink on duty," he said and grinned. "So I'll take whatever John's having."

"Gin and tonic," Dodie said. "I'll get it. With lemon or lime, Sheriff?"

"Either," the sheriff said lazily.

Cayce said, "I'll go with you, Dodie."

He opened the wide screened door and they went into the hall which was cool and shadowy and smelled as it always did of something fragrant like flowers. But he didn't get to talk to her, for a young Negro in a crisp light suit came briskly from the back of the hall. Cayce stopped and stared and cried, "Why, Sam Williams!"

Sam smiled, so his teeth flashed very white. "Hello, Cayce. I heard you were back."

They shook hands. Cayce said, "I haven't seen you since you went off to school."

Sam was old Judith's nephew, and Cayce and Roddy, Midge and Dodie, sometimes Sam and sometimes the Burke

48

boy from across the lake had made a close little band. One of Cayce's fights with Roddy had been about Sam. Roddy had made a case of it to the judge and to his mother, showing them the bruise on his chin left by Cayce's knuckle and the bump on the back of his head where it struck the pier, but never after that did he object to Sam's joining the rest of them in the long sunlit hours of a very distant childhood. Yet it seemed near, too; the only difference was that now they were adults.

Sam said, "I heard you did your time in the Army. So did I."

"Did you get through school?"

"Oh yes. I'm a chartered accountant. I'm just doing Mr. Howard's taxes."

Dodie was beaming like a fond mother. "He's one of the best tax men in the state, ask anybody. Making money, too."

"Now, Dodie . . ." he began and clapped his hand over his mouth; his eyes twinkled gaily. "If Aunt Judith heard me say Dodie, she'd have my skin." He made a little gesture of a bow and said, "Miss Dorothy."

Dodie laughed, "Come on into the kitchen, Cayce. You haven't seen Judith yet. You're one of her children, the same as Midge and me." She looked at Sam. "The sheriff's here."

Sam's smile vanished. "That's bad about the judge. It's too bad you happened to come back yesterday, Cayce."

He knew all about it, of course; everybody in the county knew it by now.

"I had a row with him, Sam, but then I left."

Sam said, "Look here, Cayce. I had a row with the judge, too, a few weeks ago. It's something I think you'll have to look into."

"Taxes?"

Sam nodded. "The judge had me come to see him. Said he wanted me to do his taxes. Well, they didn't square up. I worked a while at the figures he gave me and then I began to see what he was trying to get me to do. I brought the whole batch of accounts back to him and told him that wasn't my line."

"So," Cayce said slowly, "I've got that to straighten up, too."

"I don't know," Sam said. "Maybe other years he didn't try to falsify anything. Maybe he just thought I'd be so grateful for the chance to do Judge Moore's taxes that I'd string along with him. But I'm not that hard up for work."

Dodie said, "The judge must have been furious."

"He didn't like it," Sam said. "Take a look at his accounts,

49

Cayce. There may be some snarls to untangle and if so, and if there's interest, it may cost you plenty. But just tell the tax examiners the truth; that is, if he made fraudulent returns for other years. Maybe he didn't, I wouldn't know. See you, Cayce."

He went into the judge's library and Dodie led the way back to the pantry and beyond, to the bright big kitchen where a cookie jar had always stood on a certain shelf and somehow was always full to the brim no matter how many times grubby hands dived into it.

Judith was there. Cayce had thought of her as old Judith; he saw now that she was about Blanche's age, at the most fifty. She was slender with shining jet-black hair and a trace of something Spanish in her high, strong nose and thin lips and the deep sockets of her eyes. Cayce caught her in his arms and her hand on his shoulder was as gentle and motherly as it had been many times before—binding up cuts and scratches, rubbing away bruises with ice done up in a napkin. She was, in a real sense, the only mother he, Midge and Dodie had ever known.

"Well," Judith said with approval in her voice and a warm light in her dark eyes. "Well, now you're home to stay."

"Yes," Cayce said.

A tinkle from the pantry caught Judith's alert ear. She called, "What are you doing, Miss Dorothy?"

Cayce chuckled. Dodie and Midge were now grown-up, too, so Judith would say Miss Dorothy or Miss Margaret if it killed her.

Dodie said, "Getting out drinks."

Judith flashed across the kitchen and into the pantry. "Drinks at this hour!"

"It's all right, Judith," Dodie said. "The sheriff is here and Father said to get him a drink."

"See that you and Miss Margaret don't touch anything. I'll not have that, understand?"

"Yes, Judith," Dodie said obediently, and got out glasses. "Squeeze those limes, Cayce, will you?"

Judith said with scorn, "Besides, it would ruin your complexions."

"I haven't got a complexion to ruin."

"You *will* go out without a hat." Judith had taken over the lime squeezing with expert fingers. The trouble was that she took over the tray and the ice and marched resolutely along through the hall to the front door and there was no chance to talk to Dodie alone. At the door, Judith hesitated and looked at Cayce. "Don't you let them trap you into saying

50

anything at all. Now mind me." There was stern authority in her voice and Cayce found himself saying as obediently as Dodie had spoken, "Yes, Judith."

He opened the door for her and she walked out to the terrace. As Dodie was about to follow her he caught Dodie's arm. "Wait, Dodie. Last night you knew about those footprints. You said not to tell anybody about the scar on my foot. Why?"

She faced him, her blue eyes troubled. He could hear voices on the terrace. They were talking about Barefoot Deeler. Luke Weller was saying, ". . . no family that anybody knows about. The prison officials don't know where he went. Nobody around Tampa has seen him. Not so far as we know anyway. Nobody around Val Roja saw him yesterday, or if so, I haven't found out about it yet."

Dodie said in a whisper, "I saw those footprints, Cayce. A scar showed on them. I remembered the scar on your foot. So I destroyed as many as I could see from the path."

Cayce stared at her. "Why, then you . . ."

She nodded, "I found the judge before John found him . . ." She stopped and Cayce followed her gaze. Midge and Roddy sitting beside each other on the balustrade were directly opposite the door and watching them. Midge and Roddy could by no stretch of the imagination resemble each other, blonde little Midge with a face like a rose and Roddy, tall, dark and secretive. Yet at that instant they did resemble each other, for their eyes had the same expression of intense curiosity.

"I'll tell you later," Dodie whispered and they went out to the terrace where the men were now talking about guns.

SEVEN

"The slug," Luke was saying, "came from a thirty-eight. We got the report this morning."

Cayce knew that Midge and Roddy followed him with that guarded and watchful look as he sat down again near the judge. Judith gave the tray a push, changing its position a fraction of an inch but providing an excuse to linger and listen, too. Luke took a sip from his glass and said, "Thanks, Dodie. It tastes fine. But, of course, I don't drink on duty."

"Everybody knows that," Henry said with a smile, but he leaned forward in his chair. "Did you say a thirty-eight? That makes a hell of a lot of racket."

51

Luke Weller nodded. "That's what I thought when I heard about it. Funny none of you heard the sound of the shot." He put down his drink, having sipped perhaps ten drops of it.

Luke, Cayce thought, was nobody's fool; all that talk about not drinking on duty yet accepting a drink with great fanfare, and the fact was, he *didn't* drink on duty. It was a deliberately disarming gesture which somehow gave Cayce a cold crinkle along his skin again. Were all of Luke's seemingly friendly and candid words merely a disguise of a completely unswerving and ruthless purpose? He had always liked Luke Weller; now he found himself growing cautious.

Luke said, "Guess I'll have to take a look at all the guns in the neighborhood. Check them. Seems like that's in the line of duty."

Henry said, "My guns are in a cupboard in the library. There's a couple of rifles and one revolver. It's a forty-five, and I don't know when it's been used."

"What happened to your thirty-eight?" Luke asked unexpectedly.

"Thirty . . ." Henry laughed shortly. "So you knew all about my guns."

Luke replied with apparently the greatest good nature. "Sure. Looked up the permits."

"I see. Well the thirty-eight is in the lake all right and has been for over a year. I was target-shooting on the boat, that was before my health got so bad. My right hand was stiffening up. I dropped the gun."

Luke said softly, "Of course I'd bet on you to shoot better with your left hand than most folks can with their right," and turned to John. "You've got a thirty-eight, right?"

"Yes. I've got a rifle, too. I used the rifle one day—oh, maybe two or three weeks ago. The revolver—no, I've not used that."

"Let me look at them. I took a look at the judge's guns a few minutes ago. Roddy showed them to me. He had a shotgun, a rifle and a forty-five revolver, all present and accounted for. None of them had been used lately. Of course, my guess is that the gun that shot the judge is in the lake." Without altering his lazy gentle voice, scrutinizing the sky again as if he hoped to track down a potential rain cloud, the sheriff said, "Heard *you* had a kind of row with the judge yesterday, John."

John was reaching for his glass. He jerked back his hand. *"How did you know that?"*

"The grapevine, John," Henry said.

"Matter of fact, Zack told me," the sheriff said.

"Well," John said, "it's the truth. Yesterday morning I was burning oleanders and the judge came over and—how did Zack know?"

Luke shrugged. "He knew. Go on."

"Well, that's all there was to it. The judge was furious, holding his handkerchief over his nose so he wouldn't breathe the smoke. I got the hose and put out the fire and that made him madder than ever and he went home. I guess the smudge is as bad as the smoke, especially if anybody has a bad heart."

Cayce asked with surprise, "Did the judge have a bad heart?"

Roddy lighted a cigarette with composure and replied. "He had one or two—the doctor called them flurries. Seemed to be his heart. Nothing serious but the smoke from burning oleanders might have been bad for him. The plant is poisonous, fumes from it are likely to give anybody a bad reaction."

"It didn't hurt me," John said.

Probably you were on the windward side. Wearing gloves . . ."

John looked indignant. "I always wear gloves when I do any chores around the place. Spiders and thorns. And poison plants I don't know anything about!"

Luke said, "Burning oleanders is a bad business, John. Might have killed the judge."

John stared at Luke, "Do you mean it might have given him a heart attack?"

"It could have, I guess," Luke said. "Anyway, he thought so."

"But I just wanted to get rid of some of them. Too rank a growth. I cut some down, waited until I thought they were dry enough and then burned them. Didn't hurt me," John said again.

The sheriff gave up on finding a rain cloud in the pearly sky and looked at nothing. "Well, the judge didn't die of a heart attack. I don't know as I've got it straight about that piece of land you're living on, John. I know that you and—" he nodded at Cayce, "Cayce's father were friends. I know you were together when he died . . ."

"We weren't together. He was in a communications center, while I was in a forward unit with a radio, probably hiding behind a hedgerow, and half the guns around me had stopped."

"We all knew why you came here, John—you and Cayce's father had planned it that way. Did Lawrence Clary or the judge or anybody ever give you the deed to that piece of land?"

"No! I'd have bought it but the judge said it was all right to build on it and stay as long as I liked."

"If that land isn't yours, John, why did you fence?"

John stared at the sheriff. "Why, because I wanted to. It's not all fenced. . . ."

"Most of it," Luke said. "All you've got to do is run a few yards more fence between that and the Clary east grove and it would all be fenced."

Henry seemed to move his right hand involuntarily as if to stop something he saw coming. John said, "But why not? It wouldn't hurt anybody."

"Now, John," the sheriff said, "you're a lawyer. You've been living on that place for more than seven years. Close to ten years as a matter of fact. You get that all fenced and pay the taxes and it belongs to you. That's squatter's law."

John said slowly, "I did pay the taxes. Every year since I came here. I felt that I ought to do that and the taxes didn't amount to much. But I paid because I wanted to. That land's not mine. I put my cottage on it, sure. Lawrence, and the judge too, said it was too low for trees, no use to them. Neither of them suggested paying rent. When I came here after the war because—because there was nothing else for me to do and Lawrence had told me to try it—the judge said to go ahead and build on the land. I could stay there as long as I wanted to. But that land is not mine!"

The sheriff said, "Somebody made you an offer to buy it, though. Isn't that right?"

"Yes. I told him it wasn't mine. I couldn't sell. How did you know somebody had offered to buy it?"

"Things get around," Luke said. That was true enough; there was a most accurate and remarkable grapevine binding that close community—unless, on occasion, it tore it violently apart. "Couple from the north, man and his wife wanted a place on the lake. Asked Jenkins at the Val Roja gas station who owned the land. Only strip unimproved is the place you're living on. Jenkins told them. Land is high around here now."

"I didn't shoot the judge in order to sell that land . . ." John began hotly.

"Nobody but the judge would be likely to stop you. Cayce wouldn't have objected."

John got up and sat down again. "Now see here, Luke! I wouldn't try to sell something that's not mine to sell!"

Luke sighed. "Look's like I'm kind of riding you, John. But there's something that strikes me as kind of peculiar, so I'd better ask you about it."

54

"Go ahead," John said.

Cayce saw that Judith had gone quietly inside the house but was standing very still just inside the front door, her white dress outlined against the dusk of the hall. Sam was now standing beside her, listening too. Well, why not?

Luke said, "You said that you didn't see anybody else on the lake, didn't hear a motorboat, didn't see anybody around when you found the judge, John. No gun. Nothing. Seems kind of remarkable."

"But that's the way it was," John said simply.

Henry Howard said, "Luke, if you're going to accuse everybody that quarreled with the judge . . ."

The sheriff cut in, "That includes you?"

"It certainly does," Henry said. "And everybody knows it."

"You and the judge on bad terms?"

"We weren't on any terms! The last time I went there he showed me the door."

"Now why was that?"

"It's a long story, Luke, and I've got a notion you already know all about it. The sum of it is the judge was a bad neighbor. He didn't take care of his groves. Our groves adjoin. Any parasite or blight in his groves traveled to mine. The specific cause of last year's quarrel with him was that visitation of Mediterranean fruit flies we had for a while. The state got busy right away and got the groves sprayed; it was stamped out, practically before it got started. But the grove owners had to get on the job, too, to lick the thing. The judge didn't. I could still get around then. I went to talk to him and while I was there I told him what I thought of the way he was letting Cayce's property go to pieces."

"Is that all?" the sheriff asked.

Henry waited a moment before replying. "No," he said at last. "I told him he had driven Cayce from home. I told him he ought to get out and turn Blanchards over to Cayce."

"He didn't like that," the sheriff said mildly.

John put down his glass with a thump. "I'll tell you something else he didn't like, Luke. I had some words with him, too, about Cayce's property."

"When was that?"

"Well—several times, if you want to know. The place was going downhill so fast. I asked him about it—just a question or two, when I had a chance. He finally told me it was none of my business and—to tell you the truth . . ." he stopped.

Luke said, "The real cause of your row with him yesterday was that?"

55

"Well," John said, "we've not been very friendly lately. But I didn't shoot him."

"Somebody did," Luke said. "I guess I've got to talk to you, Cayce. Let's go over to your place." At the steps he added mildly, "And you too, Dodie."

Cayce flashed a glance at Dodie and her browned face was suddenly very still. The crimson lipstick on her mouth seemed to stand out. She said, however, coolly, "All right, Sheriff. In a minute." She put her hand on her father's shoulder. "Can I give Cayce some of your clothes, Father?"

Henry chuckled. "You certainly can. His shirt's going to split right up the back any minute. You've filled out, Cayce."

"See you, Henry," Luke said pleasantly, nodded politely at Midge who was sitting bolt upright like a Dresden doll frozen in an attitude of puzzled alarm, and ambled down the steps and out of sight behind the lugustrums.

Dodie went into the house, a flash of green and yellow and slim brown legs. Roddy looked across the lake. Midge said sharply, "Why do they want to talk to Dodie?"

"She saw Cayce yesterday right after he talked to the judge," Henry said, and after a moment, "Go with them, John. Tell that fat Luke Weller that you've got a right to be present."

"I don't know that that's a very good idea." John emptied his glass in a thirsty gulp, set the glass down and stared at his bare brown knees. "Looks as if I've got on the wrong side of the sheriff. Oleanders! Fences!" He looked at Cayce. "I'm not trying to steal your land."

Cayce laughed. "That piece is not worth stealing, John. But you're welcome to it."

Roddy extended one long arm, dropped an ash over the balustrade and said softly, "Cayce is the big landowner now, isn't he?"

His silky voice was again like the judge's voice but Cayce was hardened to that; what he didn't like was the little secretive smile on his face. It could mean nothing; Blanchards now belonged entirely to Cayce and he could do with it as he chose, but nevertheless the secretive little smile bored into his consciousness like a worm and stayed there.

John said suddenly, "Luke doesn't know everything!" An expression of almost gleeful canniness flashed into his face; it was transparent as a child's look when he suddenly discovers an advantage in a game.

Henry eyed him sharply. "Don't try any tricks, John.

56

Luke's no fool, don't try to pull anything. You'd only get yourself—and Cayce," Henry said shrewdly, "in hot water."

"I don't know what you're talking about," John said with such an air of injured innocence that Cayce felt his nerves tighten uneasily. But then John said soberly, "If you should really need a lawyer, Cayce—I mean I'll do everything I can for you—but if you should need somebody else, get Charles Penn. Charles Penn—remember it. He's a good man."

Roddy plucked a leaf from the lugustrum and examined it minutely. Midge eyed her basket of camellias. Judith and Sam had vanished from the doorway. Henry sighed and said, "Why did it have to be yesterday, Cayce, the very day that you came home? After six years why couldn't you have stayed away just another day!"

Cayce said unexpectedly, "Maybe that's why it happened yesterday." He had not until that moment thought of such a possibility, and it came out abruptly. Roddy dropped the leaf he held. Midge turned, her lovely face blank, and stared at him. John said, "Why, what do you mean, Cayce?" and then jumped out of his chair. "Somebody knew Cayce was here! Knew he had had a row with the judge! Knew the police would say that Cayce had murdered the judge . . ."

"Wait a minute," Henry began and Roddy cut in, smooth as a knife going through butter. "You knew Cayce was here, John. Dodie knew he was here. Nobody else except Zack. I was away from the house. My mother was away from the house. The judge hadn't said a word to either of us about expecting Cayce to come."

Cayce said, feeling a little flat, that that was true. "The judge didn't know I was coming. I just got on the plane and came. Nobody knew I was coming."

Dodie came flashing out of the house again with a stack of clothing over her arm.

Dodie and Cayce and John walked along the terrace together. There was no chance to ask Dodie when she had found the judge, or how it had happened, for the sheriff's car was unexpectedly close. He nodded when Cayce explained to him John's presence. "No harm in that," the sheriff said mildly. "Anyone wants a lawyer can have one."

The contrast between the Howard place and Blanchards was even sharper as the sheriff's car shot out of the lane between the Australian pines. They went directly to the study.

The sheriff sat down. "I may as well tell you right off, Cayce. I saw Zack again this morning. Fact is, he came to me. He's kind of mad because you fired him, but all the same

57

he's got some ideas that—say, a jury might cotton to. Now he'd already told me you were here and he'd sneaked up to the window there just as you said you'd come back after the judge was dead—and that sounds mighty like a threat, Cayce. That's all Zack knew; he says he just heard that and went away again. He says the grove men were in the south grove and left at five prompt. He says the judge usually came out to the sheds or walked around the place between five and six o'clock. Zack says he waited because he wanted to talk to him about a tractor they were having trouble with. He says he heard Miss Blanche and Roddy come home between five-thirty and six. He thinks closer to six. He got tired of waiting so he came and looked here in the study but the judge wasn't here. Zack says he walked across the lawn just to take a look and see if the judge was fishing. He says he went only to the edge of the lawn and he didn't see the judge's body. But what he did see—Cayce, have you got a scar on the ball of your right foot?"

There was no use in denying it. "Yes," Cayce said.

"The fact is we found another footprint. This was in the grove and it wasn't scratched out. There's not much of it showing, just the ball of the foot as if somebody was going along on tiptoe, but right across the ball of the foot there's something like a scar." He turned to Dodie, "Why did you drag brush over those footprints near the path, Dodie? On account of that scar?"

Dodie said, her voice as clear as a bell, "Did Zack see me?"

The sheriff nodded. "Says he didn't see the judge's body and he couldn't have if he went no further than he says he did; I walked down that far and tried it. The pier gets in the way. But you can see part of the path and he says he saw you, Dodie, bending over, there on the path, and you had some brush in your hand and Zack says it looked as if you were—well, sweeping is what he said. Says he thought you'd lost something. He didn't see the judge, didn't see anybody but you, came back and asked at the house for him. Roddy said he hadn't gone fishing and the car was there so he must be around somewhere. Zack went back to the tractor and smoked awhile and he was there when John came to the house to tell him he found the judge. But you'd found him before John did, Dodie." The sheriff's bright eyes were very stern. "Why didn't you tell anybody? Why didn't you report it?"

Dodie flashed one odd look at Cayce, odd because there was something appealing in it. She said steadily, "Yes, I found him. He was dead. It—it was horrible. I started home. I was going to tell Father, have him call the doctor or you. I don't know what—I guess I was scared. But then I saw those footprints. So I brushed them out." She looked at Cayce. "I'm sorry I missed that one in the grove, Cayce. That is, I knew they weren't your footprints but I didn't want anybody to see them. And—I'm sorry that I didn't tell you—I was going to tell you but I didn't know where you were and I couldn't write to you and I was going to ask the judge if he knew where you were but somehow I couldn't. Then yesterday afternoon the time was so short—I was going to tell you though, right away. That's why I told you to send me your address."

Cayce moved to Dodie's side as if something had pulled him. But she turned toward the sheriff. "You can't make me give evidence against Cayce. I'm his wife."

After a long moment Cayce caught at her shoulder and whirled her around. "Dodie, what do you mean?"

Her blue eyes were very direct. "It's true, Cayce. I found out only a month or so ago. I drove up to Georgia just to—to make sure. I never really trusted the judge about anything and—well, he just didn't have our marriage annulled. He said he did. He told my father and you and me and—but he didn't."

The dark polished teakwood floor seemed to dissolve under Cayce's feet. He said the first words that came to his lips. "My Lord, Dodie. You might have married and had a batch of kids by now."

"Well," Dodie smiled, "so might you."

He'd never thought of marriage, a real marriage, not a childish, impulsive and quickly ended elopement—to anybody but Midge. He said, explosively, "No!"

Somehow he knew that Dodie guessed his thoughts. Her brown face tightened. "Of course, I'm not really your wife. Only legally."

"But my gosh, Dodie," the sheriff said dazedly, "that's important."

EIGHT

Dodie turned to the sheriff. "Cayce can have it annulled, or I can have it annulled, any time we want to. But not till this is over. Understand that, Sheriff?"

The sheriff rubbed his nose with an air of frustrated perplexity. "I understand you'll refuse to testify. That is, if I should ask you to testify. I haven't asked you yet."

"You're inquiring about those footprints. Is that footprint you found in the grove clear?"

"Well, yes and no," Luke said with his air of disarming candor. "It's clear enough to see that there's something that looks mighty like a scar across the ball of the foot but the land is hummocky there and—" he glanced at Cayce, "it's all grown up to weeds. Looks as if it hadn't been harrowed for a long time. This footprint was on a bare patch of soil which was wet from the shower. But the State Police say we might get the bare footprints of everybody in the county and still not be able to identify this print precisely."

Dodie said calmly, "Then that's all right, Cayce."

"But all the same," Luke said, "we're going to try. And it does like like a scar right on the ball of the foot and Cayce has got a scar there."

"Luke, why would I run around in bare feet if I intended to kill the judge?" Cayce demanded. "Why would I take such a chance with a scar that would lead anybody right straight to me?"

"Because you remembered Barefoot Deeler, you knew he was coming out of the penitentiary . . ."

"I didn't know it!"

"It was all in the papers. And, the point is, you had forgotten that scar. . . . That's right, isn't it?"

"Roddy told you that! He asked me. I haven't exactly forgotten it but I hadn't thought of it for a long time."

"It's natural to forget a scar. I've got a barbed-wire scar across one knee. Damned near tore my leg off when I was a kid but I hadn't thought of it for maybe fifteen years—not till I saw the mold of the footprints the State Police made."

"All right," Cayce said. "Whoever made those footprints wanted something like a scar to show but nothing else!"

The sheriff said with unexpected mildness, "Maybe, maybe." He turned to Dodie. "The scar was good and clear on the footprints you found, wasn't it? So you destroyed them and you didn't report the murder and you've withheld evidence . . ."

"I'm Cayce's wife," she said.

My wife, Cayce thought, incredulously. It was preposterous —mainly because she was Dodie and he could not reconcile her with that new role. She felt his look, for a little pink color came up under the tan in her cheeks, but she wouldn't look at him.

The sheriff sat back in his chair. "Now why would the judge lie about that annulment?"

Because it was exactly like the judge, Cayce thought; the

60

judge had not annulled the marriage as he said he had done simply because in the wily inner working of his mind there had grown an intention somehow, sometime, to use that fact. Probably the judge himself didn't know just how and in what circumstances he might be able to use it; it was only his instinct to store up ammunition.

The sheriff suddenly came up with a different answer. "Of course, the judge knew that Dodie would be a rich girl sometime," he said with an apologetic glance at Dodie. "The judge wouldn't have minded getting all that money in the family."

Dodie said coolly enough that the sheriff might be right. "I thought of that, too. I couldn't think of any other reason for it. Nobody who didn't see him every day, Sheriff, knows the kind of man the judge was. He didn't beat Cayce when he was a boy. Cayce was well fed and clothed and given shelter and sent to school. There was never anything that you could put your finger on, could quote. But he was cruel all the same and he hated Cayce."

"Why?" Luke asked.

"For the same reason. He wanted money and he wanted Blanchards," Dodie said quietly.

John said unexpectedly, "She's right, Luke. In the public eye the judge was a fine citizen. The fact was he made Blanche's life a hell. He drove Cayce from home."

The sheriff rubbed his nose again thoughtfully. "The judge seemed to get along all right with Roddy. Of course, Roddy stayed here, I suppose, because his mother wants him but I always thought too it was because the judge needed him to help with the groves."

Dodie said, "Roddy knows nothing of the groves and cares less."

"Maybe," Luke said, "but he'd have no interest in the judge's death. In fact, if Roddy wanted to live here, he'd have every interest in keeping him alive. Unless the judge had something to leave."

He had leaped a gap ahead of any of them with startling rapidity. John said, "Did the judge leave some money? Well, of course, he must have left something and it probably goes to Roddy."

"I haven't found out yet whether or not the judge made a will. Miss Blanche doesn't know and Roddy says he doesn't know. If he left no will, Miss Blanche is his next of kin. And, of course, indirectly Roddy would be his heir, too. The point is how much—or if—the judge had anything to leave anybody." He turned to Cayce. "Why did you think the judge sent for you, Cayce?"

"I told you. I thought it was to talk over business affairs. But the only direct thing he said was to ask me to stay here for a few days."

Dodie said, "I think I ought to tell you, Sheriff, the judge had had a sort of queer experience a week or so ago. Before Cayce came."

"What was that?"

"He was out in that light skiff of his, fishing. Old Stinker —I mean an alligator that has been in the lake a long time— all at once attacked the boat and knocked it over. The judge couldn't swim, he never could swim. Besides, he was always talking about his heart. He yelled and floundered around and Roddy heard him and got him out."

There was a long silence. Then the sheriff said, "Now that's funny. Alligators don't usually go for a boat like that."

Dodie said slowly, "I don't think it was the boat. You see —after they got the skiff to land later that evening, I looked and there was a board, a piece of light timber on the end of the boat, upright so it would stick down into the water. It was splintered up to about three inches below the water. And of course even Old Stinker would go for a smell of blood."

The sheriff rose. "Good heavens, girl, are you trying to say that somebody fastened some chunks of meat on that timber, tied them on or nailed them on in the hope that the alligator would upset the boat and the judge would drown or have a heart attack? . . ." He sat down again staring at Dodie. "That would be murder!"

Dodie said, "He was murdered yesterday."

"Did the judge suspect anything?" Cayce asked.

"I think he did," Dodie said. "I certainly suspected it. That's why I looked at the boat. It wasn't like Old Stinker. And you know—alligators don't bite, they twist food off and then take it away and bury it for a while. Suppose Old Stinker lunged at the boat and twisted. It's a very light boat and it turned over. Anybody could have figured that out."

It was true; anybody brought up in the lake country knew it.

The sheriff said in a stunned way, "Did you talk to anybody about this, Dodie?"

"No, there wasn't anybody to talk to except my father and I didn't want to upset him. Though I think the judge knew it and he was scared and I think that's why he sent for Cayce. For one thing, he knew Cayce was in New York so whoever did fix that boat wasn't Cayce. And another thing, he didn't like Cayce, he hated him, but he trusted him. I think he wanted protection."

62

"Oh lordy me," Luke said. "I wish I'd stuck to raising watermelons."

But perhaps Dodie was right, Cayce thought. Certainly it would explain that impression of a fleeting sincerity that had struck him twice during his talk with the judge. He said slowly, "The judge never liked me, Luke, but if he was scared, he might have sent for me. He did ask me to stay, but he made it clear he didn't want me to live here."

"Did he hint at anything like attempted murder?"

"No. He wouldn't have confided in me. He wouldn't have asked me outright to stay because he wanted help."

"Maybe not," Luke said doubtfully. "I don't like this, Dodie. Are you sure it happened like that?"

Dodie nodded once.

John said, "Did you see this, Dodie?"

"No. It happened about sunset. Roddy got him out and up to the house and got the boat in. He was at our place that night and told me about it—Midge was in Tampa and Father was having one of his bad times and was in his room. When Roddy left I got to thinking about how odd it was and I—well, I took a flashlight and went down to the pier and looked. I don't think Roddy ever saw the splintered piece of timber or knew about it. But I think the judge did."

John said, "That lets Roddy out. He wouldn't arrange a thing like that and then pull the judge out when it worked but shoot him nine days later."

"I don't know what anybody would do," the sheriff said explosively. He eyed John for a second. "How do you know it happened nine days ago?"

"Saw it—at least I was on my porch and heard the judge yelling. I ran down to my boat landing. By that time Roddy was helping the judge up to the house. I didn't know about the alligator. I supposed the judge had slipped and given himself a ducking. . . . Look here, Luke, have you found anybody who heard the gunshot?"

"No."

"Well, I've got an idea about that." John hitched forward. "When the bombers go over you can't hear another thing and . . ."

Luke got up. "Looks like it might have been that way," he said elliptically. "I checked with MacDill Field. The bombers went over at eighteen minutes after five."

"Well, then," John said, "Cayce left here at four-thirty. Or close to it."

"That's right," Dodie said. "I looked at his watch."

Luke went to the door. "Nothing to prevent him coming

63

back . . . Cayce, they say at the courthouse that that deed was never recorded. Take a look in the safe. Try to find a will if there is one, too."

He clapped his hat on his head and went out. Dodie faced Cayce for a moment, her head high. "Don't worry about that marriage," she said clearly and sweetly. "We'll have it annulled." She smiled as coolly and politely as if she had invited him to tea. "Come over for a swim later, if you like. You, too, John." There was flash of yellow and green and very shapely, bare brown legs. Then the door closed—a little sharply, and she vanished.

But what could he have said, Cayce thought with dismay?

John rubbed a hand over his thin gray hair. "The judge ought to have had that deed recorded when your father died."

"Does it make any difference?"

"No. A deed is a deed. But, of course, it has to be recorded to have a clear title. It didn't matter then, I suppose. It was all in the family and there was no sale involved. But the property is worth considerably more now than when your father died. Land here has appreciated.

"Your groves have matured. I think you'd better have that recorded as soon as you can. Why the judge didn't record it I can't even guess except he had some kind of tricky notion. You'd better find that deed, Cayce."

But tricky or not, Cayce thought after John had gone, there was no way in which the judge's failure to record the deed could have been of advantage to the judge. On the contrary, it was to his interest to preserve it.

He looked thoughtfully around the room wondering where to begin. There was the old safe in the corner, stacked high with magazines with an electric fan perched carelessly on top of them. The desk stood opposite the French doors. The judge had not been a tidy tenant at his father's desk; there were cigarette burns and rings left by moist glasses on its green leather top. He'd start with the safe.

His father had taught him the simple combination years ago. The judge hadn't altered that, at least, for the big door opened promptly. As Cayce turned on the green desk light, adjusting it so its beam fell on the dark interior of the safe, his first look made him wince, for the safe was jammed untidily with papers. He drew out a bundle of papers which was held together by a worn rubber band, which gently snapped as he put the bundle on the desk. As he sat down, the door into the hall opened.

"Cayce," Blanche said, "it's lunch time."

That morning she wore her usual wispy kind of dress which

looked old-fashioned and limp; it was gray and had white lace on it and hung almost to her ankles. Her hair was in the same great red bun at the back of her neck, as she had always worn it, with fine wisps escaping. Her unfathomable dark eyes fastened on the bundle of papers on the desk. "Starting so soon?"

"I have to catch up on the grove records."

"Of course. I'm afraid I can't help you. Or Roddy either. The judge always kept business affairs to himself."

I'll bet he did, Cayce thought shortly. He put the bundle of papers back in the safe and swung the heavy door into place. Blanche said, "You'll need some clothes, Cayce. You're bigger than you were six years ago."

He nodded toward the stack of clothing Dodie had dropped on the chair near the door. "Dodie lent me some of Henry Howard's."

"Oh," Blanche said, "I didn't think Roddy's clothes would fit you."

Cayce repressed a fleeting grin as he saw himself burrowing under a truck or guiding a tractor clad in Roddy's elegantly tailored clothes. He said, "I'll come to lunch just as soon as I can wash up."

Blanche nodded and went away. Cayce scooped up the bundle of Henry's clothes and went upstairs. Ten minutes later, his hair wet from the shower, he went downstairs again. The clothes had included some blue linen shorts, below which his legs looked indecently white. The sun would soon correct that. As he went along the hall he thought, with a start, of the office in New York; he must telephone or wire, and explain the situation.

It was an odd lunch perhaps because Cayce had the repeated impression that Blanche was trying to talk to him and finding it hard going. She spoke of the weather, she spoke of Midge and Dodie. "Neither of them has married," she said, "and they're both so attractive. It's not for lack of chances, I'm sure. Don't you find them attractive, Cayce?"

"Very," Cayce said. Dodie, his wife!

She talked briefly of the judge's funeral; Thursday was the day she had selected; that suited Roddy, did it suit Cayce?

He wouldn't have expected to be consulted. He agreed briefly.

He didn't like sitting in the dining room with the judge's armchair, once his father's chair, so markedly vacant. He didn't like sitting in that room from which so many times he had fled trying to hold back angry and helpless tears after a tongue-lashing by the judge—while Blanche sat and looked on and made no move to check the judge or to salve the feelings of a sometimes almost frantic boy. He said, "I'll take my coffee in the study."

"Certainly, Cayce." She touched the bell and told the maid to take Mr. Cayce's coffee to the study. But by the time he had opened the safe again Blanche came to the door. "Cayce, I forgot to tell you. People may be calling this afternoon. You know, it's sort of the custom around here. I think you'd better see them."

Blanche had always had a rigid regard for conventions. The judge had been murdered and the police suspected Cayce of having murdered him, yet Blanche wanted him to take his place by her side when people called. He said, "All right, I'll be on hand."

The house was very quiet and the study was very hot. He turned on the electric fan, which stirred up the bundle of papers on the desk. He was prepared, in a measure, for disorder; he was not prepared for the miscellaneous, unfiled and uncharted mass of bills, receipts, old letters, forgotten advertisements which were stuffed, without any regard for value or records, in the safe. It would take weeks to go through all of it. He did not find checkbooks or check records; he did not find any income tax records. More important, he did not find the deed to Blanchards. At length he shoved the accumulation back into the safe.

His father had given him a key to the desk, too, years ago. It was a kind of symbol of Cayce's place as his son whom he trusted, and although Cayce had never in his life opened the desk, he had kept the key constantly on his key ring as a reminder of his father and a kind of talisman, a promise of his return to Blanchards sometime.

He wondered again if the judge had changed the lock but he had not and the desk opened at once. There were the checkbooks, there were the income tax carbons and there were the bank deposit records. Half an hour later, Cayce knew the full damning truth.

He leaned back in the worn old chair. His hands were grimy with dust. The electric fan sent a purring breeze over his sticky, hot face. His first paralyzed thought was strange: how could the judge have been such a fool?

There was only one answer to that and it was because the judge thought he could get by with it. He had hoped to put off the accounting he must have known Cayce would demand sometime. He had thought he could trick the income tax examiners and that nobody could touch him, Judge Moore.

And in the meantime he had milked the groves for all they were worth and, if Cayce's first survey was right, had reaped a very substantial fortune. It was deposited in two banks, in his name, and from the looks of it he had also a very tidy account with his broker. All of it, every penny of it in the judge's name.

Yet he had known that sometime Cayce would demand an accounting. He had even asked Cayce to stay—but briefly, believing he could stave off too pressing questions on Cayce's part. Or had the judge got in too deep and wanted Cayce's help? Cayce doubted that. It was easier to believe that the judge was so certain of himself and his power over the boy Cayce had been, that he was sure he could continue to deceive him—and rob him.

It was barely possible that he had intended to make some sort of deal.

Had he evolved some agreement which would permit the judge to leave Blanchards, and let Cayce take over, so the judge could retire to live on the money he had milked from the place and leave Cayce with Blanchards, laden with debt and no cash in the bank for repairs and running expenses?

Somehow that didn't seem likely. The judge would have known that in transferring the place to Cayce, Judge Moore would have been asked for an accounting.

Dodie's explanation seemed the more reasonable in the light of his new knowledge of the judge.

A woman's light footsteps tapped along the straw matting outside the corridor. Blanche opened the door as he swung around. "People are coming, Cayce."

"I'll put these papers away and come out."

She nodded and went away.

Cayce stuffed all the bankbooks and records back in the desk. And he thought unexpectedly, how did Blanche really feel about the judge? John said the judge had made her life a hell. Was John right? She had always seemed to agree with him but suppose, in her heart, she had hated the judge too? His thoughts raced on too quickly showing him a picture of a woman in a dowdy, old-fashioned dress walking quietly and resolutely down to the pier where she might have known she would find the judge and then as quietly, unseen by anybody, returning to the house. She would be shocked and grieved when she was told of the judge's death, but composed.

Perhaps it was that composure that conjured up the ugly picture. There had to be a motive for murder and Blanche had no motive—unless she had, in fact, hated the judge.

But, of course, he now knew that there was a conceivable

motive! If the judge had left a will, leaving all the money he had taken from Blanchards to Blanche and thus indirectly to Roddy, that was a motive for murder.

Yet all his knowledge of Blanche rejected the frightening picture that had sprung into his mind. And besides, she and Roddy both had alibis for the presumable time when the judge had been murdered. It might be a dubious alibi with Blanche swearing herself blue in the face to protect Roddy, but its very weakness, to Cayce, gave it support. If Blanche had quietly determined to kill the judge, she'd have provided herself with a less questionable alibi. Wouldn't she?

He heard a car drive into the circle outside. He opened the study door; there were voices in the living room, properly subdued. He took the quick way through the kitchen and up the back stairs, he washed and put on a fresh shirt, and then came down the front way to greet his neighbors and take his place beside Blanche as host of the house.

Roddy, however, was already there standing close beside his mother, his handsome face set in grave and decorous lines.

Someone said, "Why, Cayce Clary! We heard you were back."

NINE

Everyone said that in the same high, soft, drawling voice over and over again; their smiles did not hide the speculation in their eyes. They had heard he was back and they had also heard that he was all but accused of the judge's murder.

There were not really many people there, yet it seemed to him that the room was crowded. He spoke to old Mrs. White from Suncas City and could not fail to note her uneasiness, the way her keen old eyes darted over him and then away again, exactly like a chicken unsure of its quarry. She moved away from him as soon as she could. Mrs. Burke made her way to him. "Cayce, my dear," she said warmly, "it's good to see you. I'm sorry it has to be at such a time." She shook hands warmly, too, as if she meant it. "Bill is in the air force now. He's stationed at MacDill Field."

Bill Burke had been younger than the rest of them; Cayce remembered him as a thin, sun-tanned boy in his teens. Cayce said, "That's nice he's so near home."

Suddenly Mrs. Burke's good-natured eyes had a faint misting of tears. "They're saying terrible things about you, Cayce. Don't let them."

Her husband, changed very little except his hair was gray and Cayce remembered it black, came up and put his hand firmly around his wife's plump arm. "We must be going." He nodded shortly at Cayce, and went to speak to Roddy. He lingered there, patting Roddy on the shoulder.

Well, he'd have to expect it, Cayce thought. Until it was proved in a court of law who killed the judge, he was suspect.

Dodie appeared at his side. She was wearing a simple, pale blue dress and she looked very feminine and beautiful; he thought again, with utter incredulity, why she's my wife.

If Dodie shared his thoughts, she gave no sign of it. She said, "I saw old Joe Burke. Pay him no mind." There was a little laugh in her blue eyes as she deliberately used the embracing and pungent Southern phrase. "Father's over there."

Henry was in the front of the room, sitting with dignity in his wheel chair. Cayce didn't know whether Dodie led him to Henry or he went of his own accord; in any event, Henry saw him and drew him to his side. He kept him there, obviously friendly, showing all those people, Cayce thought with gratitude, that he for one did not believe for an instant that Cayce had shot the judge. Midge was talking to Roddy, accepting the tiny glass of sherry the maid served. Her expression was suitably grave but her bright, kitten's eyes saw everything.

And then it was over, for people were drifting out to the porch and down to the shabby circle before the house, stopping to say good-bye to Blanche and Roddy. Cayce himself was eyed covertly and a little nervously. Only Henry Howard said, as Cayce and Joe Burke together lifted Henry's wheel chair down the steps and onto the level driveway, "Come and see us, Cayce."

John's cottage was not visible from the porch, too many trees, too much shrubbery intervened. Blanche said, "I wonder why John didn't come."

Roddy laughed shortly. "John! He knew he'd get nothing but a glass of sherry, if that." He lighted a cigarette. "Well, that's over. It was quite a turnout really."

"People thought well of the judge," Blanche said in an oddly thoughtful way.

"They were thinking of his murder! They could hardly wait to get away and talk about it. Or, should I say, talk about us?" Roddy said smiling. He turned to Cayce. "I hear you spent the afternoon going through the judge's papers. You might have waited for me."

"Why?"

"Why, because I—that is, Mother—must be the judge's heir."

And it might mean a long legal fight. Cayce needed that money which the judge had accumulated from the groves. But this was not the time to fight. Cayce said temperately, "I needed the groves' records. . . . I'm going over to the Howards', Aunt Blanche."

Roddy hesitated, then he came down the steps after Cayce. Halfway along the drive he said, "I wouldn't get in a hurry about things, Cayce."

"What do you mean by that?"

"Oh, that's all." There was a complacent little smile on his mouth.

It worried Cayce out of all proportion to what Roddy actually said. Cayce really didn't want the money for the money's sake; he thought he could say that honestly; but he did want it for Blanchards. He had a little money saved but it would be barely enough to meet the payroll for a few weeks. He must get this nebulous and perplexing situation cleared up and he must find a way to draw on some of the reserves of cash deposited in the judge's name.

The girls were already down at the pool. Midge wore a white bathing suit that was so delicate and graceful it looked like a party dress except that it was cut off short above her pretty knees. She was sitting at the edge of the pool, becomingly framed in the azaleas behind her. Dodie was splashing vigorously in the water; Cayce could see only her wet dark curls. Henry was on the terrace. Cayce said, "I'll come down in a minute, I want to talk to Henry."

"Running for help already?" Roddy asked.

It was spoken in the judge's taunting voice and, mysteriously, it rolled off Cayce like water off a duck's back. He went up to the terrace and Henry said, "Come on, sit down, Cayce."

"Look here, Henry, I think I'm in trouble."

A wry but amused smile touched Henry's face. "That's putting it mildly."

"Besides murder I mean. . . . I've been going over his papers this afternoon. The judge has put away the income from the groves in his own name. Apparently he had put just as little money back into the groves as he could for several years. I looked for the deed to the place and haven't found it. Didn't find the judge's will either. Roddy and Blanche are his next of kin so it doesn't really matter whether or not he left a will."

70

Henry took it all in promptly. "That will mean a court fight, Cayce. Your father's intentions were clear. But you can't tell what a court will do. I don't think Blanche and Roddy are likely to give up easily."

"There's another thing. Mind you, I've had only a quick look at things and everything is in a hodgepodge. But it looks very much as if there's going to be a sizable income tax affair to straighten up."

Henry nodded. "That doesn't surprise me. Did Sam say anything to you about that this morning?"

"Yes. That is, he said the judge had hired him to do his taxes but they quarreled."

"That's not all. The judge offered him a bribe to juggle the figures. That's what it amounted to. Sam was smart and saw through it and refused. But a thousand dollars is a good chunk of money."

"The judge's income from the groves must have been pretty substantial. I saw his bank deposits and broker's account."

"These have been good years in Florida. Expansion everywhere. Good prices for citrus fruits," Henry said.

Down at the pool, Midge laughed; it was a musical sound as delicate as the trill of a mockingbird. Roddy apparently kept swimming trunks in the cabaña, for he was poised on the diving board, tall and slender, his black head outlined against the lake, wearing black trunks. He shouted something and made a dive as expert as that of a fish. Dodie was floating along beside a red and white rubber raft. Somehow he knew that she was watching him and Henry on the terrace.

Henry said, "I'd take one thing at a time, I think. Wait and see what Luke decides to do."

"Henry, are you trying to say that Luke Weller really thinks I killed the judge?"

"I don't know what Luke thinks but I know he's got to get an answer."

"Arrest somebody?"

"Arrest the murderer. He'll not charge anybody with this murder unless he thinks he's got a case."

"I'm the choice so far."

Henry said suddenly, "Who do you think killed the judge, Cayce?"

Cayce rose and went to the balustrade. Down at the pool Roddy was ducking Midge and Midge was protesting and laughing quite as if there were no such thing as murder, or suspicion of murder.

Curiously, Blanche's face, with those still, unfathomable

71

eyes seemed to float between him and the lake, pale and fixed, regarding him steadily. After a long moment he said, "I don't know."

Henry said, "There are several ways of looking at it. The judge could have quarreled with somebody who simply ended the argument by shooting him, on an impulse, without plan. Knowing the judge, we can't rule that out. It's equally true that the judge was the kind of man who makes enemies; one of them might have planned to murder him for a long time and—something perhaps happened that set off the trigger. But by and large there aren't many motives that are so urgent and so deeply personal that murder is the only recourse. One of them is money," Henry said quietly. "Another is fear. Another is simply hatred."

"I always thought I hated the judge. Certainly I quarreled with him but . . ." He turned to face Henry directly. "It's queer, Henry, but I don't hate him now. And I don't think that I ever hated him enough to kill him. There were times when I was a boy when I would have liked to punch him in his teeth. But that's not like killing."

"I believe you. But there's the money motive. That's what people are thinking of. I don't mean money literally—I mean possession of Blanchards."

"Zack would be a strong witness for the prosecution."

"Why did you fire him?"

"You heard about it?"

"Oh, yes. The grapevine. This time it came by way of Joe Burke." He nodded toward the Burke place, shrouded in its ghostly gray Spanish moss, lying directly opposite them across the lake. "He heard it in Val Roja. Zack was talking. He's got a loud mouth, you know. Said you'd fired him and you'd wish you hadn't."

"I had to, Henry. I went out this morning and there they were, he and the grove men, lounging around, doing nothing. Zack tried to put me in my place so I fired him."

"A good thing in the long run," Henry said. "It's a pity though that it had to happen just now."

Midge called from the pool, "Cayce—come on . . ."

Henry said, "It wouldn't hurt to talk to John about the money the judge salted away. He'll keep your confidence and he'll know something of the legal angle. I think your father did more for John than even we know. John has talked to me. He was in a suicidal frame of mind when he and your father got to know each other. Lawrence was an idealistic man and

72

yet he always tried to put his ideas into action, so in that way he was practical, too."

"He let the judge pull the wool over his eyes," Cayce said, "but he always thought the very best of everybody. He wasn't fit to cope with the judge."

Henry said, "Have the reporters been after you yet?"

"No," Cayce said, startled. He had not thought of that.

"They will be. Some of them were here today. I talked to them. . . . Go on now and have a swim. Forget all this for a while. Besides, if I don't send you down there Midge will have my hide."

But Dodie is my wife, Cayce thought unexpectedly. He ought to tell Henry the situation; he hesitated and remembered that it was not his secret alone, it was Dodie's too. He said, "Thanks," and trotted off down the lawn.

Dodie saw him coming and thrust a brown arm out of the water. "Come on in, the water's fine," she sang in their old chant and added practically, "There are swimming trunks in the cabaña. Second door."

There were dressing rooms, showers, even a tiny kitchen with a refrigerator. He found trunks, shed his own, or rather Henry's clothes, got into the trunks and came out. Dodie met him. "Cayce, have you seen John?"

"No. That is, not since this morning. Why?"

Her gaze went past his shoulder toward the end of the lake and he turned to follow it. From there they could see John's tiny landing strip and his one boat drawn up and tied.

Dodie said slowly, "Usually by this time there's a light in his house."

There was no light showing there behind the mass of green.

Neither of them heard Midge's little bare feet on the concrete behind them. She said, "Why worry about John? He's drinking. You'll not see him for three or four days."

TEN

There had been changes and many of them in the six years just passed, Cayce thought soberly as he made a slow easy dive into the pool. He had thought so much was the same but he was wrong; there had been changes.

He and Dodie and Midge and Roddy, Sam Williams and, of course, the young Burke boy had all grown up; that was

73

to be expected. The six years had fixed the judge's character traits the more firmly; that was to be expected, too. Henry had been ill; he was all but crippled yet in a way that might have been expected; that or something like it for Henry was, by no means, a young man.

The groves had changed; that was a physical change, something that could be seen. His groves had gone downhill; Henry's groves had flourished. Now that he knew what the judge had been doing with the money from the grove, he understood it.

But how about the changes in people, changes which didn't show?

Dodie was sitting at the edge of the pool; Cayce swam over to her and hoisted himself up beside her. "Is this a habit of John's? Disappearing for days on a drunk?"

Dodie gave him a troubled look. "He has done it a few times. He just stays in his cottage and nobody who knows goes near him and then he seems to pull himself together."

Cayce stared down at the water and thought of John's arrival at Blanchards. It had been preceded by a letter to the judge and the judge read the letter to Cayce; it was one of the few times when the judge made a kind of pretense of consulting Cayce. The scene was so clear that it seemed to be superimposed upon the placid water of the blue-lined pool. The judge had summoned Cayce to his study. "I have a letter here. It's from John Tyron. You may remember that your father spoke of him frequently in his letters."

Cayce had nodded; he had remembered every word of his father's letters.

The judge cleared his throat in a faintly deprecatory way. "Your father—well, he was not a worldly man, perhaps. In any event you may remember that he said in one letter—I think I have it here—" he nodded at the safe, "that he had convinced this Mr. Tyron that it would be an excellent plan for him to come to live here. Your father's plan was for Mr. Tyron to use that low land on the other side of the east grove. He's a lawyer; he has had some sort of tragedy in his life and Lawrence's idea seems to have been that he could make a new life for himself here." The judge tapped John's letter on the desk; his heavy red eyebrows were lowered. "Lawrence was, of course, very sentimental. Not that there's any harm in that. But I do feel that I may have been a great help to your father in—shall we say, a business way."

Cayce hadn't known how to answer that; there was a sting in the judge's words, yet as so often it was hidden and veiled; Cayce felt that there was something he wished to dig out and make an issue of in order to defend his father. Yet, some-how, there was nothing to dig out.

The judge had gone on. "The point is, even though your father is dead, this Mr. Tyron wishes to take him up on his offer. Impulsive," the judge had said, shaking his head a little, "but, of course, kind-hearted." He looked directly at Cayce. "What do you want to do about this?"

The judge so rarely asked for Cayce's opinion that Cayce was deeply surprised. And again he didn't know what to say.

The grown-up Cayce, staring down at the water, could see the fifteen-year-old Cayce trying not to wriggle in the maroon armchair, trying to be sober and sedate and manly. That Cayce had said, "If Father wanted him, let him come, of course."

The judge eyed him and said, "That land is no good for crops, it's waste land, really." He put down the letter. "Why yes, Cayce. You're quite right. Your father's wishes should be carried out by all means."

Even then Cayce had thought, why was the judge so agreeable about this? And then he had known the answer; it was waste land and no good for crops, yet the fine, public-spirited judge would receive a certain credit in the community for permitting John Tyron to live there, his head kinsman's wartime friend.

So John had come. It had been an event in Cayce's life, the arrival of this man who had known his father in those last years of his life.

Dodie had been very silent, almost as if sharing his thoughts. But she said suddenly, in a low voice, "Cayce, that marriage, you know . . ."

She wouldn't look at Cayce; she splashed her slim feet in the water and watched the spreading rings.

"Our elopement?" Cayce said, grinning a little because it was so unlike Dodie to show embarrassment about anything.

"Father doesn't know. Midge doesn't know. Nobody knows. Let's keep it that way. After this is over we can have it annulled very quietly. But none of them ever need to know."

Cayce said, "You're very determined to get rid of me."

All at once Dodie was natural again. She snapped, "Oh, don't tease me!"

"The sheriff knows about it."

"He'll not tell anybody. I saw him this afternoon. He was walking around that place down by the pier where the judge was found. I asked him not to tell anybody. He said he wouldn't unless he had to."

"He won't unless there is a trial." Cayce heard his own voice, stiff and cold and at the same time incredulous. He, Cayce Clary, on trial for murder!

Dodie glanced at him quickly. "There'll have to be an inquest. Maybe he was thinking of that."

An inquest, of course! "I forgot the inquest. Has the sheriff set any time for it?"

"He didn't say. There's Father." She got up with a swift graceful motion, putting her wet cool hand on his shoulder for an instant as she rose. Henry, in his wheel chair, accompanied by the little thump of the motor, was coming swiftly down across the lawn. Cayce scrambled to his feet and went with Dodie to meet him.

The turf was so strong and springy that even the passage of Henry's heavy chair made only a brief mark upon it; Cayce absently watched the tough grass spring up again in a matter of seconds and thought that he must ask Henry what kind of grass seeds to buy.

Henry checked the chair precisely and said, "I forgot to tell you, Cayce. It's been an unusually dry season. Don't forget to water."

"Father," Dodie said, "there's no light in John's cottage."

Henry's eyes traveled swiftly down to the end of the lake. "Well—I wouldn't worry about it."

Blanche was waiting for them, still in the dowdy, limp gray dress, when he and Roddy went home through the swift twilight. There was little conversation during dinner; there had never been much in the way of communication among the three of them but then the judge had always been there, talking if he wished to talk, so they were all obliged to listen or at least make a pretense of listening. After dinner Roddy said he was going to Val Roja for the papers, Blanche said she had a headache and was going to bed, and Cayce strolled down to the old fishing pier.

He leaned against one of the weathered old piles at the end of the pier and smoked. The lake, as always at night, was faintly lighter with the reflection of the sky but ringed by such impenetrable shadows that if he had not known its irregular boundaries, he could not have guessed just where there was a muddy shadowy inlet or just where a thicket of mangroves made its stubborn way out into the water. There was still no light in John's cottage. He ought to do something about John, sitting there in the dark drinking. But what? He was debating what to do when to his relief a light sprung up on the porch of the cottage.

At the same time car lights shot out from the driveway above, glanced over the house with its mass of bougainvillaea and turned toward the garage. It was, of course, Roddy, returning from Val Roja with the newspapers. He went up to the house, met Roddy at the study door, led the way into the study and turned on the desk lamp.

"I suppose you want to see the papers," Roddy said, smiling. "However, they haven't treated you too badly."

He spread the papers over the desk. There were headlines, of course. Prominent citizen slain. There was a long story of the murder. There were even some paragraphs devoted to Lawrence Clary and his war service—culled, Cayce knew, from the accounts of Lawrence's death ten years back. He then found his own name, Cayce Clary, as kin of the murdered man, returned the day of the murder after being away from home for six years. If there was an implication that something more than coincidence might explain the judge's murder on the very day of Cayce's return, it was only that. Roddy was watching him, his dark eyes amused. "They wouldn't want a libel suit on their hands, would they, Cayce?"

Cayce folded up the papers and handed them to Roddy. "I expect Aunt Blanche will want to see these."

"No news to her," Roddy said lightly. "She saw the reporters this afternoon early. You were working in here, she told me. She told the reporters you weren't at home."

Cayce stared at him. It wasn't like Blanche who never made a decision but left it to the judge. "Why did she do that?"

Roddy shrugged. "I don't know. Maybe she thought you'd say too much. My mother," he said slowly, the gleam of amusement gone from his eyes so they were cold and dark, "my mother does not believe in washing dirty linen in public. She doesn't realize that murder is everybody's business."

"Roddy, I didn't murder the judge. It would simplify everything if you'd believe that. It happens to be true."

"It happens to be what you say is true," Roddy said. He looked at the safe. "I think we'd better get some things clear, Cayce. Next time you want to go through the judge's papers, I want to be here. My mother and I have a certain claim." He put the newspapers under his arm and walked out and up the stairs.

Cayce rose early the next morning, before anyone else was about. The sun was touching the trees with gold when he went out to the shed. He had the water tank filled and attached to the small tractor when the two grove men drove up and got lazily out of their car. But they followed his orders that day with a show of briskness.

It was nearly noon when the sheriff arrived, and a police car arrived with him. Cayce, watering the east grove, saw them and went to the house for what proved to be a rather grim little ceremony, and that was a cast of his own footprints.

"If Dodie hadn't destroyed those other footprints we might have identified them," Luke said, after the police car departed. Cayce was standing beside Luke's battered little car, and Luke leaned against the car, took off his hat and wiped his forehead. "As it is, we've got to take everybody's footprints. But I honestly don't think we're going to get very far. The only thing that seems fairly certain is that the one print is too big to be a woman's."

"But those footprints—I mean that business of a scar —that's phony."

"Figure it that way, do you?"

"Luke, a man with a scar on the same foot where I've got a scar—running or tiptoeing through the grove in bare feet, but taking good care to leave an impression of just the ball of the foot where the scar would show—do you really believe it could have happened that way?"

Luke's sun-wrinkled face was turned toward the lake, his eyes squinted. "Don't know just what I believe."

"If it's phony, then somebody did it purposely to involve me."

"Can't prove that, can you?"

"Of course not. But it's reasonable."

"Maybe," Luke said. "Well, I've got to go and see John. Get his footprints. He's the only one left on the list."

"You mean—all the people around here . . ." Cayce had an odd, sickening sensation, as if a net were closing invisibly around him, shutting off air.

Luke got into the car and started the engine. "It isn't likely a perfect stranger walked up and shot the judge." He idled the engine and said thoughtfully, "If Dodie had been a few minutes earlier when she went down to the pier, or if John had been earlier when he rowed over this way, we might have had a witness. Two of them, in fact. I don't know. I've questioned both of them, but maybe I've not hit on the right questions. I keep thinking . . ." He shoved his hat back on his head. "I keep thinking that maybe one of them saw something or heard something that didn't seem important, and still doesn't seem important, but might *be* important. . . . Did you find that deed?"

"Not yet."

"Find anything like a will?"

Cayce shook his head. "I'll get back at the papers this afternoon. I had to get some watering started."

"Yes, I guess so," the sheriff said slowly. "But the groves won't do you much good if we have to charge you with murder, Cayce." He drove away and Cayce stood watching the car until it disappeared behind the Australian pines. Then he walked absently back into the house and into the study.

The house seemed very still, so he heard the little bang of the front door, the tap of high heels along the matting outside the study, even the soft rustle of a skirt. Midge opened the study door, blinked in the half-gloom and said, "Good morning, Cayce. I saw the police leave. Miss Blanche went into town with Roddy this morning. We haven't had any time alone together, Cayce, and I want to talk to you."

ELEVEN

She was already in the room, light and graceful as a butterfly, but very smart too in her sleek yellow dress which clung like a sheath; she perched like a butterfly too, on the desk. "I'm so glad you've come home to stay. I began to think you would never come."

He'd been wrong to think of her as a butterfly; the sheath-like yellow dress was like the calyx of a flower, designed to show its perfection. He said, "I'm home to stay, if the police will let me."

Midge's eyebrows went up. "You mean they may arrest you? That's the silliest thing I ever heard of!" She laughed, and it was as musical as the first bird songs in the early morning.

He waited for his heart to turn over, but rather disconcertingly it didn't. "The sheriff and the police were here just now," he said. "They were taking casts in the hope of identifying that footprint."

"Oh, I know that!" She laughed merrily, as if it were all of a kind of game. "They were at our house this morning, too. Why, they even took Father's footprints and he hasn't been able to walk for over a year. They took mine, too," she said with almost an air of pride, sliding one of her small feet out

79

of its slipper and eyeing it. It was extremely delicate and graceful. "They looked sort of disappointed.

"Cayce, darling, you've been out in the groves working like a common laborer. I saw you on the tractor. You don't have to do that. Why, goodness me! You own Blanchards now. You can get all the grove men you want."

"It's not that simple. Grove men have to be paid."

"But there must be all the money you need or want. The judge spent just as little as he could. I suppose he was saving it for you."

He was saving it all right, Cayce thought grimly.

Midge swung her little foot idly and looked at it and said softly, "I suppose you're really what you'd call a rich man now, Cayce. Owning Blanchards and everything."

Cayce thought of the absurdly small balance in the bank in New York, which he hoped to string out as long as he could. "I'm not rich."

"Oh, Cayce, if that isn't just like you! You were always so cautious. Funny—I know that about you but nobody else does. They all think of you as—well, sort of a wild boy—just because you ran away from home, I guess." Midge's long eyelashes lowered. "Now you're back, everything's the same again with us, isn't it, Cayce? The way it always was with you and me."

Cayce felt as if suddenly his collar were too tight, and then realized his collar wasn't fastened. Suddenly, too, the study seemed suffocatingly warm. "But—Midge . . ."

"You're thinking about the judge's murder, aren't you? That will settle itself, you'll see. Think about . . ." She gave a soft little laugh, came close to him and put her fragrant lips against his face. "Think about me."

"Midge, I'm already married."

Midge's head jerked back. "I don't believe it."

"Well—it's true."

"Who is it? Some girl up North? Well, you'll just have to tell her you made a mistake and . . ."

"It isn't some girl up North. It's Dodie."

Midge caught her breath sharply. Her whole lovely little face changed subtly, as if a wind had rippled a lake; yet strongly, as if that wind had stirred up life which had been concealed under a placid surface. "I just don't believe you! Dodie never said a word."

"It's true," Cayce said doggedly, "all the same."

Midge's eyes flashed. "That elopement! But that was annulled."

"No, it wasn't."

80

"Oh," Midge said. She looked at him for a long moment. Then she said, "But of course it *will* be annulled. Dodie will see to that." She laughed and went out through the French door. He had a glimpse of her yellow-clad figure, her shining blonde hair against the azaleas, and then she vanished.

Cayce stared at the green wall of azaleas without seeing it for a moment, took a long breath and dived again into the stacks of papers.

Blanche did not return for lunch and he was still at the table when the sheriff telephoned. "The coroner decided to have the inquest this afternoon. We made it short notice purposely. At three o'clock, at the courthouse in Suncas City. I've already phoned to Roddy in Tampa, and he said his mother'd been in Tampa late this morning but was on her way home, so you tell her when she gets there, will you, Cayce?"

He had showered and dressed when Blanche came home, and he went down to meet her. She was pale and tired-looking. "It was hot in Tampa," she said. "I drove Roddy's car home. He'll get a ride with somebody later."

"The inquest is this afternoon," Cayce said. "At three."

"Oh." She looked at him blankly and then put up a gloved hand to the heavy red knot of her hair. "Of course. The inquest. The sheriff said it might be today, but they hadn't fixed the time yet. What will they do?"

"Bring in a decision of murder, of course." Suddenly he felt sorry for her. "Have you had lunch?"

She told him yes and that it would take them thirty minutes to get to Suncas City, and went upstairs slowly, dragging herself along, one hand on the railing, the other carrying a dress box. At the top of the stairs she turned and looked down at him. "Cayce, when do you want Roddy and me to leave your house?"

She looked white and tired, with her thick red hair wispy and untidy and her body sagging against the railing. Unexpectedly his heart smote him. He could not say, "Get out of my house now."

But he could not believe his own ears when he heard himself say, "This is your home, Blanche. It's always been your home."

Immediately he was appalled at what he had said. Blanche made a tentative step downward. "But, Cayce—do you mean that?"

"This is your home," he heard himself say in a clear, rough voice. "We'll have to hurry, Blanche."

"All right," she said, after a moment. She disappeared in the hall above. And Cayce thought, now they're here forever,

81

Blanche and Roddy both. From the hall she called down to him and oddly her voice didn't sound like Blanche, for there was a sort of firmness and lift to it. "We'll take Roddy's car. It's already out in the drive." Her bedroom door closed.

Cayce stared down at the mahogany railing beside him for a long moment before he struck it with his closed fist. Why had he done that? Simply because she had looked so tired and because she'd lived there so long. No sensible reason. Nothing. He went out to the porch and stood staring with blank eyes out over the lake. All right, he thought at last; I said she can stay, but that doesn't mean that Roddy can stay here, too.

He went down to the car which stood in the circle, and got into it.

Roddy had done himself well with the car; it was new, glittering, luxurious, powerful—Cayce whistled softly. Roddy must be getting a handsome salary from his Velidas relatives. Of course he had lived at Blanchards and he had to pay only, Cayce supposed, for his clothes, club fees, dinners for the girls he took out, that kind of thing. But still this car ran into money.

The front door opened and closed, and Blanche came down the steps. He wouldn't have known it was Blanche if he hadn't known it couldn't be anybody else, for she was dressed in a trim, neat black dress and simple black pumps with high heels. She wore a small and smart black hat, and her hair was very neat. She carried white gloves and a new, flat black handbag. It must have been the stark simplicity of the black that startled him, for he had never known her to wear anything but pinks and blues and grays which always somehow looked faded and out-of-date. She seemed curiously younger; even her walk had a kind of spring to it. He got out to open the car door for her and she thanked him and settled down in the front seat.

Assuredly, Cayce thought, as he walked around the car and climbed back into the driver's seat, he didn't know this woman. Had she changed so much in those six years? Again the question caught at him in an obscure, yet troubling way. Six years is a long time. He had changed, hadn't he? Well why not Blanche? Nobody remains exactly the same; things happen.

He knew well enough why that question nagged at him. He had assumed that he knew all these people thoroughly and well; he had assumed that he would know what they would do and what they wouldn't do. But that was wrong. The crux of it was that, in fact, he didn't know whether or not any of them could have committed murder.

82

He started the car, feeling an absent little thrill of pleasure at the sheer perfection of mechanism with which it moved. He had entered the shadowy driveway between the towering dark pines before it struck him that Dodie had not changed at all.

Blanche said, "Do you like Roddy's car? The judge gave it to him."

TWELVE

This startled Cayce so that the car swerved, and he steadied it. It wasn't like the judge to give anybody the sum of money that car had cost. He wouldn't even have spent it on himself, for Cayce had seen the car that the judge must have driven, standing in the garage; it was a substantial enough car, practical, certainly not new, and nothing like the fine car he was guiding now out of the shadowy lane and onto the country road.

Blanche said, "It didn't cost much really. Some friend of Roddy's—he lives in Havana—had bought this one and used it for a while and then—I don't remember, I think Roddy said that he was going back to Havana, or something like that, and wanted to get rid of this one. Roddy said it was a bargain."

There was something here that was puzzling. "How much did Roddy or the judge pay for it?"

Blanche replied at once. "Twelve hundred, I think."

Blanche believes it, otherwise she wouldn't have spoken so casually. But either Roddy or the judge, or both of them, had lied to her—that, or the Cuban friend was excessively charitable.

It reminded him of the mass of papers and canceled checks still unsorted. "Aunt Blanche," he said, "you remember the deed my father had drawn up before he went into the Army?"

"Of course."

"Do you know where it is?"

She turned to look at him, frowning faintly. "Why, I suppose it's in the safe."

"Where was the judge's safe-deposit box?"

"In the bank at Suncas City. I think he had one at Tampa at one time. But then he transferred the account to Suncas City. I don't know why."

Cayce knew why; he hadn't transferred his account, he

83

had merely started a second one. Diversionary tactics, Cayce thought grimly.

Blanche said, "Turn here. We'll come out on the new highway. It's much shorter that way."

As they approached Suncas City, sprawling beyond all its former bounds with sparkling new houses, gay in their pink and white and yellow paint, she said, "I remember the deed, Cayce. It was one of the last things your father did before he left. But I haven't seen the deed since then—in fact, I don't remember seeing it then. I just knew there was such a deed. There's the new courthouse. Turn at the next corner."

New stores now lined the streets. Plate-glass windows gleamed. Every parking space was full. Cayce turned and passed the old courthouse, red-brick, vine-covered, cramped and far too small to accommodate the civic needs of all this new, burgeoning county life. The new courthouse, when they reached it, was a palace, but a sensible palace of concrete with huge windows and simple, modern architecture. People were standing on the steps. Among them a man with a camera saw them coming and swung up his camera expertly. Cayce put his hand on Blanche's arm. "Take it easy," he said.

But to his vague surprise Blanche adjusted her hat and straightened her shoulders and paused for a second to pose.

The sheriff detached himself from the group of men and came to meet them. The camera must have clicked a few times, for the man holding it looked satisfied and lowered it. The sheriff said, "I thought we'd keep this quiet. That's why we gave such short notice. Hoped it wouldn't get around. But things do in these parts." He sighed, and added, "I guess things get around everywhere. We're no different."

A police car zoomed up and Roddy slid from the back seat and came across to join them.

Roddy, too, was aware of all those observing eyes and of the camera swung up again. He took his mother's hand and kissed her cheek very gracefully. Blanche flushed a little, as if it were an unusual gesture. "The police car brought me up from Tampa," Roddy said. "You didn't give us much time, Sheriff."

"Didn't aim to," Luke said.

As they made their way through the men standing on the steps, all of them watching, and entered the cool broad corridor inside, Luke drew Cayce a little to one side. "Didn't get Dodie over here," he said, so low that Cayce could barely hear him. "Guess I've fixed it so that part of it needn't come out right now. Besides—" the sheriff's steely eyes were neither friendly nor unfriendly "—fact is, we couldn't very well swear

84

her in as Dorothy Howard. Not when I know her legal name is Dorothy Clary."

"Oh," Cayce said. Dorothy Clary.

The sheriff said, "She told me she wouldn't testify anyway. She meant it. Dodie's stubborn." He turned toward the spacious, well-lighted room at their left.

It was crowded. A little murmur went over it as Blanche and Roddy and Cayce and the sheriff walked up the aisle to seats near the front, which were held empty and waiting for them.

Dr. Hastings, the coroner, was both formal and quietly and casually informal, and he, instead of Luke as Cayce had expected, presided.

He began with a little speech, easy and drawling, and full of colloquialisms which were as familiar to Cayce as his own bones. The purpose of the inquest was to come to a decision as to the cause of Judge Cayce Moore's death. Nothing else. He said that firmly, adjusting his gold-rimmed spectacles and giving the entire roomful of people a stern and composed glance which was so deliberate that it seemed to single out every one of them. He wore a wrinkled seersucker suit and a black knitted tie. He was older than Cayce remembered him, thinner, his hair whiter. He then said, with a casual yet commanding air, that he would call Dr. Walters to give his testimony, and explained, as if he were addressing his own family or his own patients—as indeed many of the people present had been at some time—that Dr. Walters had assisted him with the autopsy.

A young man, also wearing a seersucker suit, a Northerner by his accent and very brisk, came promptly forward, was sworn in, and told them what everybody there in all probability already knew. Judge Moore had died of a bullet wound through his heart. He described the wound with a kind of youthful zest in technicalities. He couldn't have been long out of school, Cayce thought; a few more years and the pockets of his jacket would bulge from carrying a stethoscope at all times, everywhere, never knowing when he'd be summoned from the movies, from a game of bridge, from church; a few more years and those crisp Northern accents would dissolve into an easy, elliptical drawl. Blanche listened without flinching.

"Thank you, Dr. Walters," the coroner said. "I might tell you folks that Dr. Walters and I are entirely agreed about this thing. His testimony is the same testimony I would give. Now, then, we want to establish the time of the judge's death, near as we can. John . . ." He looked down at the end of the front row of seats. "John, will you come up here please and tell everybody just when you found the judge?"

Cayce hadn't seen John; he watched as the neat, spare figure in white shirt, gray slacks and a thin gray jacket moved forward. John was perfectly sober, clear-eyed and very serious, so they were all wrong when they thought he'd been overtaken by one of his drinking bouts. He gave his testimony much as the coroner had spoken, simply and without formality.

The coroner questioned him briefly. "Did you hear the sound of a gunshot?"

"I may have without noticing. But I don't think so."

"You said a flight of bombers went over the lake about an hour before you found the judge?"

"Yes, that's right."

"So the shot might have occurred at just that time?"

"I don't know, but it seems reasonable. It is usually so quiet around Clary Lake. I don't see how I could have failed to hear a gunshot, unless it happened at just the time the bombers were going over. You can't hear anything else then."

"You say you found the judge between six-fifteen and six-thirty?"

"About that time. I can't be sure."

"Now, when you found the judge you're sure he was dead?"

"Yes," John said.

The entire room was quiet for a second or two; perhaps the one word gave a vivid picture of that moment in the dusk when John had seen something white lying there amid the reeds, and had rowed over to see if it was, in fact, what it seemed to be.

Dr. Hastings cleared his throat. "Did you see any other boats on the lake while you were fishing?"

"No. Not that I noticed. I think I'd have noticed."

"Did you see anybody near the fishing pier in the vicinity when you found the judge?"

"No," John said.

"Thanks, John. Now then—is Lieutenant Faraday here?" John went back to his seat and the coroner looked out over his gold-rimmed spectacles and then nodded as a slim young man in Air Force uniform rose. "Come up here, will you, Lieutenant?"

The boy was very serious and stood very straight and told them simply that the practice flight had been under his command and that they had passed over Clary Lake on their way back to MacDill Field at exactly eighteen minutes after five on the afternoon in question.

"You didn't happen to look down at the lake, I suppose?" the coroner said in a pleasant, almost chatty way.

The young lieutenant shook his head. "Those bombers go pretty fast, sir," he said.

After the coroner dismissed the young lieutenant, who asked if it was all right to leave and was assured that it was, he called Roddy, and Roddy told of arriving home with his mother, going out to look for the judge, failing to find him, and returning. Roddy was all courtesy and grave willingness to assist and waited, after the coroner had dismissed him, to stand beside Blanche, who was the next witness.

She was composed and prompt in her answers. She and her son had left Tampa shortly before five o'clock; they had been slowed up by the heavy traffic, but she knew that they had been turning into the Val Roja road when they heard the flight of bombers. She thought that they had arrived home about six o'clock, but she wasn't sure. She corroborated Roddy's testimony and the coroner did not question her. "Thank you, Miss Blanche. I'm sorry we had to put you through this ordeal. You needn't stay any longer," Dr. Hastings said kindly.

But Blanche came back and sat again between Roddy and Cayce. And then the coroner said, with that air of casual informality which was somehow very serious and impressive, too, "Cayce, I guess we want to hear from you now. Come up here, please."

Cayce's whole body tightened as he went up to face Dr. Hastings.

In actual fact, however, the coroner did not so much as touch on his quarrel with the judge. As soon as Cayce was sworn in, indeed, the coroner said, "Now I have just a few questions to ask you, Cayce. It'll save time maybe. You came home that day on a visit from New York. That right?"

"You, sir." There was something very keen in the coroner's eyes behind those glittering spectacles, and something very commanding, as if he wanted to say something to Cayce. Cayce groped for the message, whatever it was, and found it only when the coroner said, "Now you were going back to New York that night?"

"Yes, sir."

"Back to your job, is that right?"

Cayce knew then; the coroner was putting words into his mouth and nobody would question the coroner's authority to do so, not in that community where old Dr. Hastings was a respected kind of law in himself. So the sheriff didn't want Cayce to tell the whole story then and there. Why?

There was an ominous answer to that; because if the whole story came out the jury would be very likely to bring in a verdict of murder then and there, not by a person or persons unknown but by Cayce Clary, the dead man's nephew who had quarreled with the judge and who stood to gain by his death.

But that meant, too, didn't it, that Luke himself wasn't sure yet? The knowledge flowed through Cayce like fine wine; all right then, he'd follow the coroner's lead. He replied yes, he had intended to return to his job.

"Now then, you talked to the judge for about how long?"

"Not quite half an hour."

"Did you have any reason during that talk," the coroner said rather cautiously, his eyes still apparently trying to convey a message to Cayce, "to think the judge was—say, afraid of anybody? I mean, did he say anybody had threatened him?"

Secure in his sudden knowledge, Cayce replied, "No. We talked about the groves and the judge asked me to stay at home. . . ."

The coroner said rather quickly, interrupting Cayce, "When did you first hear of the judge's murder?"

"When I got off the airplane. I had decided to come back to Val Roja. I phoned to the Howards' and I was told of the murder then."

But then it began, a kind of buzz and murmur in the crowded room.

It was not the complete story and everybody there knew it. An angry murmur, like that of a swarm of bees, grew and swelled. Cayce felt the chill of sweat on his face. The atavistic horror of a mob hovered suddenly like a living thing over the room and at the same time it seemed to provoke itself. Then a man at the back, whom Cayce could not see, rose and shouted, "Ask him why he shot the judge!"

Like a wave, it seemed to Cayce, everybody was standing, trying to see, shouting, trying to be heard. The whole courtroom had turned into one solid voice of accusation.

Blanche remained in her place; Cayce saw that. John came struggling through the people now crowding in the aisle, to stand beside Cayce. "Take it easy—take it easy," he said, his face like a withered gray mask.

The coroner was pounding with a gavel on the table. "Order in the court. By God, I'll have order in this court or I'll tell Luke to arrest every one of you. Clear the room, Luke. Get everybody out. . . ."

88

It succeeded for a very simple reason. They wanted to hear the rest of the inquest.

The murmur died away, so the sharp pounding of the gavel could be heard. People sat down, most of them looking queerly ashamed and casting glances at their neighbors.

The coroner put down the gavel, got out a handkerchief and wiped his face. He took off his glasses and wiped them, too. By this time there was scarcely a whisper of sound in the room. He put his glasses back on his nose and looked over the room severely. "I'll have nothing like that in my courtroom. I'm ashamed of every one of you. And don't think I won't remember who you are. I know every one of you. So does Luke. Now then—Cayce, you're dismissed. Go and sit down. All right now, folks. You've all heard the evidence concerning the cause of Judge Moore's death. It is the duty of this coroner's inquest to pronounce its decision."

The decision was that Judge Moore had been murdered by a person or persons unknown, and Cayce scarcely heard it, for Luke was at his elbow urging him quietly toward a small door at the front of the room, away from the main entrance. Blanche and Roddy and John were behind them. They emerged in a narrow corridor. "There's a back door this way," Luke said, and pounded heavily along the terrazzo marble floor, leading them toward it.

John said, "I'll see you at home. This doesn't mean anything, Cayce. They just got all worked up."

Roddy drove them home with Blanche sitting beside him, and Cayce in the back seat. So that, Cayce thought, was where he stood in the eyes of all those people.

The reason it hurt so was because they were his people. Roddy said over his shoulder, "I guess Luke and the coroner were prepared for something like that. Feeling is running high. Have you got a gun, Cayce?"

THIRTEEN

The unreality of the question jolted Cayce, for it was as if Roddy had suddenly decided not to play cops and robbers, but an adult game.

"Of course I don't have a gun! I don't need a gun. Nobody's going to come around here and try to string me up."

Blanche said vaguely, "That's silly, Roddy."

And then the car swerved into the road between the Howard place and Blanchards, and Cayce swerved with it a little and thus caught a glimpse of Roddy's face in the mirror, and Roddy was smiling. So what was in fact behind that question? Cayce said, "You really want to know whether or not I had a gun when I came here, don't you, Roddy? Whether or not I brought it with me in my pocket, I suppose. Why don't you ask me outright? Why don't you ask the sheriff? I'm sure he must have searched my room before now. And the cops that picked me up didn't miss anything." Cayce remembered the quick, experienced way the State Police had slapped his pockets and his arms when they bundled him into the car at the airport. "As a matter of fact, I've never had a gun—not since I got out of the Army."

They entered the driveway, and the great dark pines closed over them. Roddy said, "People around here don't like murder."

Blanche took off her new smart hat and fluffed up the wispy red hair which clung damply to her head. "Who started that shouting? Wasn't it Zack?"

Roddy replied, "No, I saw him. It was the grove superintendent for the Putnams over near Suncas City. But he is a crony of Zack's. I told you not to fire Zack, Cayce. He's got a lot of friends."

"Then most of them were in the courtroom," Cayce said. "I didn't see many people I knew."

He wasn't going to let Roddy know how that near riot had hurt him, but Roddy knew; there was a certain complacency in his voice when he said, "There were plenty of people who knew you. Not much of a welcome home, is it?"

"All the same it's home," Cayce said, as if Roddy had flung down a challenge.

The car stopped and Cayce got out to open the door for Blanche. She said, "I'm glad you didn't get mad, Cayce. I was afraid you were going to." She went up the steps and into the house.

Cayce, as if it were a refuge, went into the study. "I'm glad you didn't get mad," Blanche had said.

It was what they all thought; what the judge had made them think, by hint, by innuendo; the judge excelled at that kind of thing. Would he never really be free of the judge?

The sun was low, so the long shadows from the trees lay within the study. He turned on the green-shaded lamp and took up the telephone, glancing at his watch as he did so. It was nearly six o'clock. He hadn't thought it was so late; the inquest had seemed much shorter than that, and in another way it had seemed very long.

It seemed incredible that he had not yet telephoned to the

office in New York and explained why he had not returned and that he was not going to return. Yet he had felt as if that entire other world had automatically dropped away from him.

He tried the office number but of course no one answered. So he tried Bob Elwell's Greenwich number; probably Bob would not have reached home yet, but he could leave some kind of message.

Bob Elwell was his immediate superior, about forty, jovial and shrewd. To Cayce's surprise, Bob himself answered.

"Cayce!" he cried. "Are you on the lam?"

It was good to hear Bob's hearty voice, although the gangster idiom he affected at debonair moments seemed, just then, a trifle too appropriate. Cayce could feel the rather sickly smile on his own face. "You must have been reading the papers."

"More than that, boy. We've had some of New York's finest in the office. At least they were in plain clothes, but they were policemen."

"What did they want to know?"

"Everything, boy. We gave you a clean bill of health. Nobody ever heard you threaten your uncle. We all expected you back the same night you left. Nobody ever saw you with a gun. Nobody knew you had a gun." Bob's voice became more serious. "Look here, Cayce, you didn't bump off the guy, did you?"

"No."

There was a little pause. Then Bob said, "Anything I can do to help?"

Cayce's throat tightened. The friendliness in Bob's voice was like salve placed on a raw wound. "No—thanks, Bob."

"How about a mouthpiece?"

"They haven't arrested me," Cayce said.

There was another pause; he could feel Bob's alert mind examining the situation. He said finally, "Well, keep in touch. Are you fixed all right for money? Well, of course you must be. Now you've come into possession of your own place."

Cayce swallowed. "Oh yes—I'm fixed all right for money. Bob, I want to stay here at home."

"You mean give up your job? Well, I thought so. That's all right. But if you do want to come back to us ever, your place is waiting for you."

"Thanks."

"Meantime," Bob reverted to his jovial, casual manner, "if you should get thrown in the clink, let me know."

After Cayce put down the telephone it seemed to him remarkable that that warm and friendly contact could be cut off with only a small click of the wire.

He went into the living room; the tray with ice and decanters and glasses was already set up, but neither Roddy nor Blanche was there. He poured himself a drink and went back to the study. There was at least an hour before dinner. That morning he had thoroughly searched the desk. He opened the safe. He hadn't looked for a safe-deposit box receipt or any notation concerning it; perhaps there had been something of the kind which in his haste and amid the confusion he had overlooked.

As the heavy door of the safe swung open, Roddy came in. He, too, had a glass in his hand. His eyebrows lifted as he saw that the safe was open.

"So that's why you were in such a hurry to get here. Well . . ." He sat down in the maroon chair and leaned back. "I'll help you. The deed is right there on top."

Roddy sipped at his drink, his dark eyes smiling at Cayce above it. After a long moment Cayce said, "You had it."

"Sure. Took it out of the safe night before last, after you'd gone to bed. There it is. Take a look."

An envelope lay on top of a stack of papers, a new envelope, unwrinkled and unworn. Cayce drew out the folded paper inside the envelope. There was a catch somewhere, he knew.

But he wasn't prepared. Nothing could have prepared him for the line written into the deed, in his father's handwriting —"With a life tenancy to Cayce Moore, his sister Blanche Moore Velidas, or the survivor."

Cayce sat down slowly, holding the deed under the desk light, staring at that line of faded handwriting—faded, but his father's writing. So Blanchards didn't belong to him, not yet.

The judge was dead. But Blanchards would not belong to him as long as Blanche lived. Blanche—and consequently Roddy—were still a part of his life and Blanchards. There was no way to get them out.

Only a few hours ago he had told Blanche it was her home; it seemed now grimly ironical.

The ice in Roddy's glass tinkled softly. Cayce looked at him. "How long have you known this?"

"Oh—years, I suppose."

"Did the judge tell you?"

Roddy shrugged. "No."

"You know the combination of the safe."

92

"I've known that since I was a kid. I found out for myself. It wasn't hard to do. I have a key for the desk, too, if you're interested. I watched my chance, got the judge's key one time, and had a duplicate made."

"It's too bad you didn't go in for a criminal career. You seem to have a talent for it."

Roddy's dark eyes were dancing. "You'd like to knock my head off, wouldn't you, Cayce? It wouldn't change anything."

The first shock-wave was subsiding; it would return, Cayce knew, along with bewildering incredulity, but just now he felt suddenly quite clear and cold. "That's not the first time, then, you've explored the safe?"

Roddy said lightly, "No. And the desk."

"So you knew what the judge has been doing with the money from Blanchards."

"Stealing it, of course. If you like direct words."

"You admit that?"

"It doesn't matter what I admit here and now. There's nobody else hearing it. You'll have a hard time proving he took that money, Cayce. I suppose you'll take the whole thing to court. Perhaps I don't have to remind you after this afternoon's experience that you can't tell just what may happen in a courtroom. And besides, this life tenancy business is hard to define."

"My father's intent is clear."

"But the money is in the judge's name. My mother and I are his next of kin. You can't get around that."

"I'm going to try," Cayce said.

"I thought so." Roddy's thin, aristocratic face became sharp with intention. He put down his glass and leaned forward. "How about a compromise?"

Cayce waited a moment, studying Roddy. Finally he said, "You think I'd win in a court fight."

"I think it can be settled this way, by compromise. You get some; I get some. We don't have a long court battle to pay for. Everything settled quietly between us."

Roddy rose and came to the desk. The lamp shade made greenish shadows on his handsome face, with its thin, rapacious nose and mouth. "They're going to charge you with murder, Cayce, as sure as you live. You're going to need some money to hire lawyers and fight it. You can't wait to get this thing settled through the courts. You're up a tree, Cayce. Might as well settle with me. Private agreement. Nobody needs to know a thing about it."

Suddenly Cayce's hands tingled with a desire to strike

93

Roddy across his handsome, smiling face. Nothing could ever be settled that way. He said, "The judge knew that you knew what he was doing with the money."

Roddy eased his collar and laughed, but rather unsteadily. "For a minute I thought you were going to hit me, Cayce."

"Is that why the judge gave you that car?"

"Of course the judge knew that I knew all about it. If he wanted to give me that new car I wasn't going to refuse it."

"How much money have you blackmailed him for?"

"Not a pretty word, Cayce."

"Blackmailer and second-story man—you'll go far."

Roddy's white teeth showed in a smile which was more like a snarl. "But I'm not going to be arrested for murder. I'm not a suspect. I saved the judge's life only a few days ago. His boat was upset in the lake and he can't swim. I pulled him out but I could have just let him die in the lake. Why should I kill the goose that laid the golden egg? If you want to put it crudely, the judge was worth something to me alive."

"Get out," Cayce said.

Roddy picked up his glass and backed away. "All right. There was murder in your voice just then, Cayce. If Luke or the coroner or those people this afternoon in court had heard you just then . . ."

Cayce laughed. "I'm not going to murder you, Roddy. But if you don't get out of here I'll throw you out. I mean that."

Roddy left. Cayce was still smiling when the door closed. But all the same there was no ground for that momentary, fine sensation of being in control of the situation. The fact was that Blanche and consequently Roddy, from whom she would never be parted, were now in the place left vacant by the judge. A life tenancy—to Blanche Moore Velidas. He sat down and looked at the deed again.

Roddy opened the door and looked in. "I just thought I'd tell you. You can burn that deed if you want to. Do anything you like with it. I took it to Tampa and had a photostat made of it, just to protect Mother's interest."

Cayce said slowly, "It didn't even occur to me to destroy it. It's in my father's handwriting."

Roddy backed out the door, closing it behind him.

Cayce folded up the deed and put it back in the safe. "Stay and fight it out with the judge." Dodie had said that. All right. He was going to stay and fight it out with Blanche and Roddy.

He took the telephone again and called the Howard house. Judith answered.

"Oh it's you, Mr. Cayce. I heard about the inquest. I mean, the way those people acted. Don't pay any attention to it."

"Thanks, Judith. Is Sam there?"

"Not now. He's finished the day's work and gone back to Tampa."

"Ask him to come and see me in the morning, will you? I've got a job for him."

It was darker and would soon be dinner time; suddenly he knew he could not sit at the table in the dining room, facing Blanche and Roddy, aware now of their right to be in that room and in that house. He went out into the passage and saw Belle setting the table in the dining room; he told her to tell Miss Blanche that he wouldn't be home for dinner but to leave something in the refrigerator for him, and went back through the study and out the French doors.

There was a faint, pink light still in the sky. The lake was obscured by deep, blue shadows along its boundaries, but there was a pink reflection of the sky in the flat water out beyond the fishing pier. He walked slowly along the driveway beneath the deep shadows of the pines.

When he reached the Howard place it was lighted and Midge and Dodie were coming to the house from the pool. They were walking a little apart, yet there was a curious air of close agreement and understanding between them. Cayce could not have said how he knew that, nor why the knowledge gave him a sheerly instinctive wave of apprehension.

Midge had the faintest, smallest smile on her pretty lips; she looked as smug as a kitten over a cream jug.

Dodie wasn't smiling at all. She saw him first and stopped, and Midge turned and cried, "Cayce! I'd hoped you'd come."

Dodie waited until he was so near he was aware of her quick breathing and the deep resolute blue of her eyes. Then she said evenly, "I'm glad you came tonight, Cayce." She took a long breath. "Midge told me that you had told her that I'm —still married to you. I just wanted to say, so Midge can hear it, that I'm going to get an annulment right away. That's all," Dodie said, and started for the house.

Her dark head was high. Her slim, brown legs marched away resolutely. Her white shorts and white shirt outlined her figure in the half-dusk, glancing in and out of the occasional patches of light falling from the house.

Midge came closer and linked her arm within his arm. "I told Dodie that you and I have wanted to be married ever since we were children. Of course she wouldn't want to stand between us."

Cayce was only dimly aware of the soft but firm pressure of her white arm, and of extricating himself from it. He ran across the lawn toward that resolute, marching figure with its

95

proud head high. Dodie knew he was coming. She stopped and turned to face him. "You could have waited to get engaged to Midge! You could have waited until you didn't have a wife!"

"Dodie . . ." He didn't realize he had put out his arms toward her until she struck at his hand and turned and ran toward the terrace. He caught her at the steps and pulled her back into his arms, and held her warm and struggling against him. His whole being seemed packed with things he wanted to tell her, yet nothing was clear and conclusive; there was nothing to say. Henry's voice broke through a kind of barrier around himself and Dodie.

Henry said, from the shadowy terrace above, "Come up here, Cayce. They found Barefoot Deeler. He's in Miami and he's been in Miami ever since he got out of prison."

FOURTEEN

He followed Dodie up onto the terrace. She went into the house and Midge strolled up on the terrace, too. She sat down near Cayce, where the light from the window behind her fell across her, and listened, very demure and very pretty, still with a kittenish kind of smugness about her.

It was true, Henry told him. The police had found Barefoot Deeler and he had a hard and fast alibi and he laughed when they questioned him about Judge Clary. "He said, 'That old . . .'" Henry deleted the next words because Midge was there, and went on. "'I'm glad he's dead but I didn't kill him. I wasn't near Val Roja and I can prove it. I never thought of killing him.' That's what he said. They took a cast and he's got no scar on his right foot."

So that ended that lead, but it had been a tenuous one at best, nothing that Cayce really believed in.

"I hear there was a little trouble at the inquest," Henry said.

The grapevine as usual had operated. Somehow in Suncas County tales were borne on the breeze, whispered among the trees. Cayce laughed. "They must have a setup for smoke signals at the courthouse."

Henry laughed, too, indulgently. "Things get around. This time it was Sam Williams. He was at the inquest. Of course Zack and his friends started that. But all the same," Henry's voice sobered, "we've got to get you in the clear. We can't just let the thing die for lack of evidence. If nobody is ever

96

brought to trial and convicted, if Luke has to give up—and he's a bulldog under that lazy manner; he'll not give up easily —but if he does have to give up and there's never a trial, you'll have a bad time living here, Cayce."

Everything Henry said was true. "People around here have long memories," Cayce said.

Henry said, "Get some drinks, Midge, will you?"

Midge crossed in front of him and went into the house, moving into the hall as lightly as a flower in the breeze.

There was a moment or two of silence. Bands of light fell across the terrace, alternating with bands of deep shadow, touching the vines and shrubbery to sharp black and white. It was now full dark, except for a faint light still lingering out in the middle of the lake. All around the house the trees stood silent and black, reaching into the scarcely less dark sky and, as always at night, the scents of flowers were heavier and sweeter. A tub holding a gardenia shrub stood just beyond Henry's chair, in the light, so its creamy blooms looked very white and its foliage very dark and glossy. A warm current of intimacy seemed to flow between Cayce and Henry, sitting there in quiet and in the dusk, while he told Henry of the deed and Blanche's life tenancy.

"That's bad," Henry said, when Cayce had finished that brief story. "You're going to have to fight it. But I'm afraid you can't accomplish anything in the way of getting Blanche out. I think she's there for life and that means Roddy too. I suppose what your father really meant to do was to insure a home for Blanche in the event the judge predeceased her."

"I know. Roddy offered to settle out of court, split the money between us.'"

"What did you say?"

"No dice."

Midge came out, carrying the tray. And presently Dodie came out, moving very quietly into the shadows. She was wearing a simple white dress with a scarlet belt and scarlet, high-heeled slippers. She sat down in the shadow of the vines.

Cayce stayed to dinner. "I told Judith that you'd be here," Dodie said in a chill but very polite little voice.

The spacious dining room, with its shining mahogany, the silver on the sideboard, the long, flowered chintz curtains at the windows—all of it was like a homecoming to Cayce. There was a portrait of Henry's wife on the wall opposite Cayce and he knew the portrait, although he had never known the woman who posed for it. He had felt always a kind of bond between himself and Dodie and Midge, motherless, too, as long as he had known them. He thought Midge must look like her mother, delicate and fair. Yet the woman in the picture had very steady dark blue eyes which now—as always—seemed to read and study Cayce.

It was like a homecoming, too, because a kind of pact seemed to establish itself around the candle-lit table: nobody spoke of the judge. Henry always liked to talk, and when Cayce touched the intricate silver carving of one of the great candlesticks near him and said he remembered that, Henry said, yes, those candlesticks had survived the Civil War. He then went on to draw a parallelism between the grove owners of modern times and the planter class of pre-Civil War times. In many ways, he said, they lived the same kind of lives, for a grove was a self-contained unit. Life for the planter class before the Civil War had reached an apex of luxury, which was dignified, yet simple and charming too; in many ways the grove owners lived much the same kind of life, with its grace and traditions.

Dodie interrupted him there. "It was a nice kind of life for a few people," she said.

Henry's eyes sparkled as he glanced at her. "Well, that's true enough. And of course it had to come to an end. The Civil War was one of the peaks of the industrial revolution, something that had to be expected."

Midge's wide eyes widened. "But that was long after the Civil War," she said. "That happened in Russia in the nineteen-hundreds."

Henry gave Midge an exasperated glance, which, however, softened as Midge smiled at him. He shook his head. "I don't know why I paid all that money for your schooling, I'm sure," he said. "Never mind, dear. All you have to do is look like that. And there's another parallelism right before our eyes." He addressed Cayce. "Midge is true to the tradition of the Southern belle. Just stay the way you are, Midge. That's all anybody will ask of you."

And then he proceeded, simply because he liked talking, to tear down his own theory, which he said was, in fact, all wrong. The daily life of grove owners and planters might have its resemblances, but nevertheless the grove owners were entirely dependent upon machinery and upon factories and upon communication and upon each other. They were very closely a part and product of modern life. And automation, on its galloping way, was another peak of the industrial revolution.

Judith brought in spoonbread muffins, small mouthfuls of utterly delectable clouds dripping with butter; she brought in crab bisque and duck with wild rice, and at last a pecan pie. "I thought you might be here," Judith said. "You always liked that."

In the old days there had been a waitress; perhaps Henry saw the flicker of surprise in Cayce's face when Judith herself served the dinner, for he laughed suddenly and said, "With two girls around Cayce, we have to find work for them. Judith does the cooking and sees to the girls and me, and that's enough. The girls do everything else, whether they like it or not."

Midge made a charming little face. Dodie laughed and carried the coffee tray out to the terrace and Henry whirled his wheel chair briskly along the hall, disdaining any help from Midge or Cayce. "Get out some brandy," he told Midge. "Some of the Armagnac. It's in the library cupboard."

That meant that it was a special occasion. Cayce's heart was as warm as the brandy when it came. The only trouble was that while Dodie remained polite and pleasant, acted as a hostess and saw to his needs and her father's, at the same time she removed herself to a curious but very definite distance; she might have been miles away instead of only a few feet, separated from him merely by a table and a thin wall of shadow.

After they had had the Armagnac, and the glow of it was like a tiny stream of fire down Cayce's throat, Dodie made the distance a real one, for she rose quietly and went down the steps and vanished into the darkness of the lawn. Cayce, however, turned sharply and Henry called, "Dodie, where are you going?"

There was a stern note in his voice. Dodie called back, "Only down to the lake. It's all right, Father."

Henry said, "Go with her, Cayce. We are so isolated here," he added in almost an apologetic way. "I think all of us feel that. Groves surrounding us on all sides. A man could lie hidden in the swamps back there for days on end. But . . ."

But he might come back. Henry didn't say it, but the words spoke themselves. And of course it was true; they were isolated, all the grove owners, set off from the world by those wide acres of grove land and by the lake itself.

Midge came to Cayce's side with the graceful motion of a delicate night-moth, her skirts fluttering. "I'll go, too," she said.

It was very dark beyond the half-lighted terrace. The turf below their feet was tough and springy, not the soft, velvety turf of the North which has no need to resist long months of sun and heat. Cayce loved the very feel of it. Yet out of the still, black night there drifted an odd sense of uneasiness, like a hidden threat, because a murderer was at large.

Dodie had gone ahead of them. Cayce called, "Dodie . . ." and hastened his footsteps.

But then Dodie's voice came back through the darkness, clear and soft as a bell. "Here, at the boat landing."

She was standing on the platform at the edge of the lake. The Howard boats were tied below. A dense thicket of mangroves stood out in a black blotch close behind her. She said, "There's no light in John's cottage."

Oddly, Cayce wanted to snatch her away from that encroaching black mangrove tangle, as if it might reach greedy tentacles toward her, or as if something might creep from up close—too close—to that white-clad figure. The lake was an infinity of darkness, stretching into further darkness.

Midge fidgeted. "You said that last night, Dodie. But John was perfectly all right. Sam said he was at the inquest, sober as a judge."

Dodie said suddenly, "I'm going over there."

"What's a telephone for?" Midge said petulantly.

Back in the house Cayce tried John's number. Nobody answered. "I'll try Blanchards," he said. The uneasiness which had caught him in the darkened night seemed to sharpen. At the third ring Blanche answered.

"No," she said, "John hasn't been here. Where are you, Cayce? At the Howards'?"

"Yes. I had dinner here, Aunt Blanche. Has John telephoned?"

She told him no.

He hung up slowly. "Can I take one of your boats, Dodie?"

"Of course." She went to Henry, waiting on the terrace. "Cayce and I are going to row over to John's place."

Henry nodded. "Better take the little rowboat, Dodie."

Midge fluttered indecisively at the top of the terrace steps and then came back and sat down. "That's fishy," she said.

Dodie was already going down across the lawn toward the boats. Cayce thought she laughed, but if she did, it was the barest little gurgle; for when he caught up with her she had retreated again into a vast, unassailable distance.

Once away from the light, Cayce's eyes became better adjusted to the darkness. The lake itself took on a barely lighter hue. He untied the boat and helped Dodie down into it—a gesture which Dodie made quite obviously unnecessary by moving with ease to sit opposite him. "You can row," she said

100

coolly and settled herself down and tucked her white skirts around her legs.

"I didn't expect you to row!"

The boat did smell fishy. So did the lake. It was very hot and very still. They glided away from the dark patch of shadows around the mangroves, and there was only the light click of the oars and their soft dip and splash in the water. Dodie said, "A little to the left. You're going to hit the fishing pier."

He veered as the old fishing pier loomed up suddenly ahead, a darker shadow out into the lake. Once around it, he saw the lights from Blanchards shining brightly above. He dropped the oars and the boat drifted gently. The white still figure opposite him did not move or speak. Suddenly Cayce discovered that words were not going to be easy. He couldn't exactly say, Midge got me in a corner. She was talking about marriage, so I took the only way out that I could think of.

The fact was, he simply didn't want to marry Midge!

So he had changed, too, in those six years, and hadn't known it.

Dodie said, "Are you going on to see John or are we going to sit here? The boat's drifting. We'll get stuck in that swampy patch below your east grove."

"Dodie, I *had* to tell Midge."

There was a little pause. Then Dodie said, "In thirty seconds more we'll be stuck in the mud."

He knew the lake as well as she did. He let the boat drift on until the very last second, when the reeds became distinct even in the darkness and he knew the water was shallow. Then he took the oars and sent the boat with a strong drive out into the lake.

Dodie gave a clear, mocking little laugh. Cayce said, "All right. I told Midge that I was married to you. I *am* married to you. You can't deny that."

"I can't deny it," Dodie said, "but I can have it annulled . . . Look out, there's a shallow here."

He sent the boat out farther into the lake, and Dodie said in a different, a troubled voice, "I still can't see a light. I think you go straight ahead here. It's all so dark. Cayce—something has gone wrong—something about Blanchards, is that it?"

"How did you know?"

"Oh I could tell! You told Father, didn't you?"

He told her about the money, he told her of Blanche's life tenancy. Somehow in the telling the chill distance between them dissolved, and Dodie became herself again, not a chill, remote person he had once known. Her white dress and the pale oval of her face were dimly discernible, although he could fill in every smallest detail as if he could see her face clearly. There was her broad forehead, there was her generous mouth which could be so gay and also so firm, there was her straight nose. He even knew the way her ears tucked in neatly, close to her head, below the short, dark curls.

The boat nudged something, nudged it again, and Dodie said, "A little to the left. It's John's boat landing."

He edged the boat toward the landing and fastened the painter. This time Dodie let him help her as she stepped lightly up out of the boat. Her hands were cool and firm. She paused, her face lifted toward him. "You'll have to fight both of them, Blanche and Roddy. You mustn't leave Blanchards again," she said quietly, yet very clearly.

He knew then, clearly too, what he wanted. "Dodie—it's you I came home to."

She waited for a second. Then she drew her hands away and turned quickly into a narrow path, which seemed to plunge into midnight. Actually it wound its way through a dense growth of bamboos so tall that they shut off even the night sky. The bamboos rattled and whispered softly around them.

They emerged at the cleared space before John's cottage. Dodie stopped and caught Cayce's arm. "There's somebody—see, there at the corner of the porch."

He couldn't see anything at all but black impenetrable shadows overlapping each other, but above the slow murmur of the lake he heard footsteps crunch briefly, as if across a gravel path. Then the sound stopped and there was only the slow murmur of the lake.

FIFTEEN

"Stay here . . ." he whispered.

"No." She took his hand suddenly and guided him. She knew the way across the springy, tough turf, a pocket handkerchief of a lawn, to the house which then loomed up dimly darker than the night sky, and was distinguishable only because it had shape in all that otherwise shapeless darkness. Dodie pressed close to him, her lips almost against his face. "Look out, there's a gravel path here."

They had passed the house with its long, screened porch. There should be a step somewhere here coming down from the porch to the path, which ran beside the house back to a cleared space where John kept his car. He felt gravel under his feet and at once the headlights of a car sprang up beyond the cleared space at the back, out in the narrow winding road, and fanned out brightly, turning swamp and gaunt trees dripping with Spanish moss to silver and black. Against the spreading fan of light the car was sharply outlined, its red taillight glowing like a jewel. In the same instant an engine was started up, loud and fast. The car shot into motion. As suddenly as the lights had flicked on they disappeared. Cayce ran, stumbling in the utter blackness around him.

The sound of the car was already diminishing. There was only one way out of John's small piece of land and that was the narrow, winding road through lowland, and then a strip of swampland, and finally out to a country road which eventually joined a wider, paved road. This road branched, after a time, one way going toward Val Roja and the other winding on around the lake, following the vagaries of the higher ground.

Whoever was in the car had gone. Something brushed Cayce's face, a vine which thrust softly out as if to entangle him. Abruptly he was lost in a black pocket of night, with shrubbery reaching for him as if it had hands. He got out matches and lighted one after the other. The bright points of flame merely reflected themselves against the thick, green leaves surrounding him. Dodie called from somewhere beyond that tiny circumference of light. "John's car is here." She came out of the darkness, close to him. "See, there it is."

It was there, standing in the cleared space, only a few feet away from the thicket into which Cayce had blundered. It was the same small green convertible which John had had ever since he came to Val Roja. Its paint was a little dimmed from standing out through rain and weather for years.

So it wasn't John who had driven away like that, hurrying, aware of their presence surely, because whoever it was had absently turned on the lights when he started his car and then swiftly flicked them out again.

"I'd like to know who that was," said Cayce.

"I think it was Zack. I know his car."

The sound of the car was now far away and going faster, as if its driver had turned into the smoother country road. Close around them there was only a deep silence. Not even a night bird twittered. There was not the faintest rustle amid the crowded shrubbery. Cayce said, "We'll take a look in the house."

His voice sounded queer, tight and too even. He took Dodie's hand again and wished that she were safe at home. The place had an unearthly quality of stillness, as if it waited for something, as if it knew something and held its breath. There was a murderer at large, he thought.

He thrust Dodie behind him instinctively when he went up the steps, opened the screen door, and remembered where the light switch was, just beside the door. He found it and turned on lights and a long, screened porch sprang into being.

Dodie came up the steps and stood beside him. No one was there. There were the light Chinese reed chairs, the hemp rug, the bamboo blinds lining the screens and rolled up. There were ash trays and at the back, along the wall of the house, a chest of drawers, its top laden with magazines and papers. He called, "John—John . . ."

There was no answer.

It didn't take long to look through the living room, a scrap of a room with a fireplace, a bedroom, a tiny kitchen. John was not there.

Dodie stood for a moment in the kitchen, the bright light from above pouring down upon it. She said, "He's had a drink."

There was a glass, used but empty, on the table. Otherwise the tiny kitchen was orderly and neat. Dodie opened the refrigerator and looked inside. "See," she said. "He hasn't had dinner. There's some steak ready to be broiled." She looked at Cayce. "He must have gone away in his boat. I didn't notice it at the landing. It was so dark."

"If he took his boat, then he's probably rowed over to Blanchards. We must have just missed him."

Dodie closed the refrigerator. "I suppose so. I wonder what Zack was doing here."

"I wonder why he got out so fast." They went back into the living room. Both of them looked again into the bedroom, small, its narrow bed neatly made, nothing disturbed.

"What are you looking for?" Dodie asked.

"I don't know." But he did know exactly what he was looking for. The judge had been murdered. There was a murderer at large; he was looking for the dreadful disorder of murder once again.

That was nonsense, he told himself. It came out of the stillness of the night, the empty silent cottage so neat and undisturbed—it came from nowhere.

But again he telephoned to Blanchards and again Blanche answered.

"I'm sorry, Aunt Blanche. I hope I didn't wake you. Is John there yet?"

"No."

"Is Roddy there?" Cayce asked on an unexpected impulse. Again Blanche said no.

"Do you know where he is?"

There was a slight hesitation in Blanche's reply. "I'm not sure. He took his car. He didn't say where he was going. Why, Cayce? Has anything—happened?"

"No—no, it's all right. Thanks, Aunt Blanche." He hung up quickly before she could question him further. Yet it was true, nothing had happened, except Zack had been at the cottage and had fled away from it in a car without lights. Nothing had happened, except the cottage was orderly and neat and John was not there.

He found a flashlight on the long table on the porch. I'll take a look at the boat landing, he thought.

The light from the porch streamed out in a rectangular area. As he crossed the lawn he could see Dodie in one of the Chinese reed chairs, lighting a cigarette. He reached the path to the boat landing and a flashlight made glancing circles through the great thicket of bamboos.

There were two boats tied up at the little landing; the rowboat he and Dodie had brought, and another which must have been John's boat, tied at the other side of the small platform. Had it been there when he and Dodie arrived?

It had been so dark they had not even seen the landing until their boat nudged it. John's boat could have been there, unseen by either of them. He pulled it closer, playing the flashlight full upon it. There was nothing in the boat but a tin box of, probably, fishing tackle. The oars were wet. So that meant that John had been in the boat sometime after he had returned from the inquest. If he had had the boat out early in the afternoon the oars might still be damp, but they wouldn't have that sparkling fresh wetness.

But where was John?

Cayce went back through the crowded, rustling bamboos. The porch was still lighted and he could see Dodie's head bent over something, as if she were reading. She looked up as he opened the door.

"His boat is there. The oars are wet. Looks as if he's been out on the lake sometime this evening."

Dodie said, "I phoned home. I thought he might have walked over there while we were coming here. He's not there . . . Look at this." She held out a letter. "It was on the table here. I was looking for matches and saw it and I couldn't help reading it. Read it, Cayce."

It was very brief. "Dear Mr. Tyron: You told us, when we

105

inquired about the land you are using, that it did not belong to you and referred us to Judge Moore. I talked to Judge Moore, who told me that the land belonged to his nephew and that he was not at liberty to sell. But I remember asking you to let us know if you heard of a desirable piece of land that was for sale. So I wanted to tell you that in the meantime we have purchased another piece of land so we are no longer in the market. Sincerely yours, W. M. Newcombe."

Dodie said, "It's dated nearly two months ago. Why didn't John tell the sheriff about this letter when the sheriff questioned him? The sheriff as good as said that John might have fenced and paid taxes in order to get squatters' rights and then sell this land!"

"I suppose that's why. I mean, I'm their main suspect. This letter would have proved that John had no intention of trying to get possession of the land—or killing the judge to keep the judge from fighting it. The sheriff flatly suggested that as a motive for murder. So John just let him go on thinking it might be a motive—rather than clear himself at once and thus make the case stronger against me."

"Well—it did help a little," Dodie said dubiously.

"It's like John," said Cayce as he put down the letter, adding that he hoped that John would not make any further well-meant but futile attempts to confuse the issue.

Dodie said, "Did the judge tell you that somebody wanted to buy this piece of land?"

"No. I wonder if that's why he sent for me. No, it couldn't have been that. This man—Newcombe—must have told him he'd bought some other land."

Dodie frowned. "I still think the judge sent for you because he was frightened and wanted your presence around the groves for a while. He must have examined his boat—after Old Stinker went for it and upset it. If he saw that splintered piece of wood nailed to the boat, he'd have guessed, as I did, that somebody had baited it for the alligator. He knew you were in New York, so whoever did it, it wasn't you. He'd never have come straight out and told you he wanted your protection. But he must have suspected—somebody." She put out her cigarette. With surprise he saw that her hand crunching the cigarette in the blue glass ash tray was trembling a little—Dodie's hand, always so firm and resolute. She said, her eyes on the ash tray, "It wasn't Barefoot Deeler. If it wasn't somebody who had quarreled with the judge sometime but so none of us knew about it, then . . ."

"I know. Then it was somebody close to him."

106

Dodie's blue eyes lifted to meet his own. "That's what I mean."

There was a long silence. Certainly both of them were going over that short—too short—litany. Blanche or Roddy or John. Cayce himself, and Midge and Dodie and Henry Howard. Who else could be called close to the judge?

"*Zack!*" he said suddenly. "Zack was at Blanchards when it happened. He said he knew nothing about it. But he could have quarreled with the judge. Probably had quarreled with him many times over the years. I can't imagine anybody working for the judge who didn't quarrel with him once in a while. Zack has been accusing me, talking all over the county, trying to make a case against me. And Zack was here tonight. What did he want? Why did he leave like that?"

"He heard our voices, I expect. Sounds travel over the water at night."

"So he got out as fast as he could. He turned off his lights so we couldn't see his license plate. That's a dangerous road to drive in the dark. There must have been a real reason for not wanting us to see him or to know that he'd been here."

He looked around the porch wishing he could find a clue to Zack's hasty departure, for there was something deeply troubling about it. The whole place was in perfect order, so Zack hadn't made a search for anything—but what? His eyes fell on the photograph of his father and John, a snapshot, both of them in uniform, squinting in the sun and laughing. It stood, where it had always stood, on the table near the wall and was the only photograph in the cottage.

"It's queer," he said suddenly, "that John doesn't have a picture of his wife. At least I've never seen any photograph but that one."

"Neither have I. But it's not strange, Cayce. He never talks of her. I think it hurts him too much. I tried to tell him one time that he mustn't blame himself because he was driving when she was killed. But he wouldn't listen; I had to stop. Sometimes I've wondered—well, if he'd been drinking when the accident happened."

"I never thought of that," Cayce said slowly. "Poor old John. If that's it, he'll never get over it."

"He loved her," Dodie said softly. "I think, in a way, his real life ended when she died."

She looked wistful and gentle and so very sweet that Cayce went to her and put his hand under her chin and tilted her face up toward him. "Dodie, I'm not in love with Midge. I used to think I was but I was wrong."

107

She said steadily, "Midge is my sister. You always loved her. Oh, I know I didn't think about that when we—when we eloped and were married. That is, I thought about it but Midge was engaged to Roddy then and . . ." She stopped and at the quick wave of color in her face, Cayce felt as quick a wave of jubilation.

"What do you mean, Dodie? Tell me."

But his jubilation was short-lived. "You're going to ask me why I married you," Dodie said. "I've thought about that, too. I knew why you asked me to marry you. I knew it then. You were lonely and hurt and you wanted somebody. You turned to me. But we were children. It's different now."

"What would you have done if the judge hadn't separated us?"

"I don't know."

"I know. We'd have come home and lived together . . ."

"Happily?" she said. "No, it wouldn't have worked out like that."

"All right. Perhaps not then. We were both too young. I didn't even have any money. I can't remember that I gave that much thought. I guess I just supposed that Blanchards would support both of us. But now . . ."

"But now I'm grown-up and so are you. I love Midge. We're sisters. She's still in love with you. She has every reason to believe that nothing could change between you. She says that you and she are going to be married. So that's settled. . . ."

"But that's not true! We're not going to be married! Listen to me! That's why I told her about our marriage. I had to, Dodie. Can't you see?"

Dodie said steadily, "You've just come home, Cayce. Six years is really a long time. You don't know me and I'm not sure that I know you. But I do know how Midge feels about you. And I know that ever since you were a boy it was Midge who came first with you." Dodie rose. "I'm going home."

"Wait—you've got to understand . . ."

"Do you think there's any use in waiting for John?"

Dodie could be as stubborn as a mule, Cayce thought; he knew the way her little chin was set that she was going to be stubborn now. He couldn't exactly blame her for it. Too much that she had said was the truth. He said, "Let's give him another fifteen minutes," and went to a chair and took out cigarettes. What could you do with a woman when she wouldn't listen?

And what exactly had Midge said to her? Little, lovely Midge with her helpless, confiding manner—and her deadly, certain will! Perhaps Midge had always had that concealed strength of purpose but his eyes had been blinded. Well, his eyes were open now.

Dodie said, "I said I'd get the annulment right away—tomorrow—well, it'll take a few days, I expect . . ."

"Months," Cayce said wickedly. "Several months. Maybe a year."

There was a flash in her eyes. "Months, then."

"You promised not to annul it until after this thing is over with. Do you know why the sheriff didn't ask you to testify at the inquest? He said it was because you were my wife."

"I'm not your wife! Don't talk like that."

"You are my wife, so you can't testify, and I want it like that."

"Cayce," she said suddenly, "I didn't tell the sheriff or you or anybody what really happened that evening the judge was shot."

The cigarette in Cayce's hand jerked. *"What?"*

"I was afraid to," she said simply. "I was afraid that if I told the sheriff, somehow he'd make me testify against you."

"You mean, it's important. What is it, Dodie?"

"It's not important—at least I can't see anything important about it. But the sheriff would have to make me tell everything—somehow—if he knew. You see—really I came out of the house just after the bombers went over."

"Do you mean you heard that shot?"

"No. But I could still hear the bombers when I came downstairs and out of the house. I did leave my radio going, just by accident, and Midge heard it. I came down to the pool."

"Did you see anybody?"

"No. At least—well, I wasn't looking for anybody. I was thinking—I just walked down to the pool and then I went out on the boat landing and sat there for a while."

He interrupted. "How long?"

"I don't know. I just don't know. But then I—I decided to take a swim. I went into the cabaña and got into a swimming suit and then I went in the pool. I don't know how long I stayed there, either. But I could tell by the sun that it was getting late when I got out. I showered and put on my clothes again. And—well, it was *then* that I started to the fishing pier and got my fishing things. I must have passed the judge but I didn't see him; there are all those reeds and brush and I guess I was still just—thinking. Looking down at the path, you see. I hadn't seen you, Cayce, in all that time and I knew I had to tell you about our marriage and I . . ." She took a long breath and said with a kind of defiant honesty, "I was thinking about that. When I came back along the path I looked out across the lake and it was then that I saw the judge."

He understood why she had not told the sheriff. "You were almost an eyewitness. The sheriff would have had to make you tell the whole thing."

"Can he make me do that?"

"I don't know. But he'd have to try. . . . What did you do then?"

"I didn't tell him the truth about that either. I saw those footprints on the way back to the house . . ."

Again he interrupted. "Were they there when you went to the pier?"

"I don't know. I've tried to remember. I can't. I told you," she said, "I wasn't looking at *anything!*"

"What did you do then?" he asked after a moment.

"I went to the cabaña. After I'd tried to scratch out those footprints. They did show something that looked like a scar, Cayce. And I—was terrified. I knew what they would say. And if the sheriff ever found out that I was so near when the judge was killed—I know, I *know* he'd make me tell a jury the whole thing. And it sounds as if—" she swallowed hard and said, "It would sound as if I knew that you had killed him. That's what a jury would think. It was all I could think of while I was there in the cabaña. I decided I wouldn't tell anybody because they'd say I must have seen whoever it was that killed the judge and that I was trying to protect whoever it was and it was you, because I'd scratched out those footprints. And now it's too late to tell the sheriff the truth."

"How long did you stay in the cabaña? What were you going to do?"

"I didn't know what to do. After a while—I don't know how long—I heard men shouting and I knew they had found him. I went up to the house and nobody saw me."

He rose and went to the screen and stared at nothing. Finally he said, "You are an eyewitness only if you saw the murder."

"I didn't see that. I didn't hear the shot."

"Did you see anything—or hear anything? Anything at all that was—different?"

"No," she said and stopped so sharply that Cayce could hear her quick breath. He turned and she was staring at him, her blue eyes huge and dark.

He was across the room. He caught her hand. "Dodie, what?"

But after a long moment she looked away from him, out

110

into the dark beyond the screen where insects, attracted by the light, were buzzing and circling. Her gaze followed a huge night-moth, all orange and black and blue, as it traveled up and down the screen. Suddenly she said, "It was nothing, Cayce. Take me home."

"Dodie, you do remember something you heard. Or saw. Something that frightens you. Tell me."

But abruptly she turned to him, young and frightened and stubborn. "Not now, Cayce. It may mean nothing. And—no, I've got to think about it."

"It's something that might threaten somebody else! Is that it?" His thoughts were racing. Dodie would protect him if she could, or Midge, or Henry.

"Take me home," she said.

She was very near him and unexpectedly disarmed and childish. He put his arms around her tight and hard. "Dodie, I wish you'd listen to me and believe me. I've changed, of course I've changed. I used to think it was Midge and perhaps it was true then, but now . . ." He stopped, for he could feel the steady current of resistance growing in the warm, slender body he held tight in his arms.

He thought, there is no gateway to maturity; there is no line that is crossed. Maturity is like a maze, one path leading to another; it is like a great building full of corridors, one turning into another. Did anybody ever reach the end, so there was a clear way ahead, so he could say, now I am rich with knowledge, now I know all the answers?

But he did know that he needed Dodie for all his life to travel along that maze with him.

Dodie said, in a small, tired voice, "Don't talk to me about that any more, Cayce. I'm going away after this is over." She drew away from him. She was a thousand miles away. He couldn't touch her or make her hear.

In fact, of course, she only walked across the porch and out the door, and he followed. When he got out upon the scrap of lawn, full into the light streaming from the porch, he remembered that he hadn't turned off the lights. It didn't matter, of course; it was a trivial thing. Certainly John would soon come home.

He caught up with Dodie at the black thicket of bamboos. John's boat was still tied at the landing platform. They rowed back, past Blanchards where there was a single light in the hall. As they rounded the jutting end of the fishing pier, Dodie said in a low voice, absently, as if she were debating with herself, "It may mean nothing. I mean, that evening the judge was killed. I've got to think about it."

He, too, spoke in a low voice, as if something on the lake might hear him. "Don't do anything silly, Dodie. Murder is —dangerous."

They approached the shadowy blotch of mangroves that marked the beginning of the Howard land.

SIXTEEN

Henry and Midge were waiting for them, Henry with a highball in his hand and Midge sitting in the light from the long window behind her, coolly knitting on a mass of pink yarn. John had not been there and they had heard nothing from him.

"Are you sure it was Zack's car?" Henry asked Dodie.

"I think so. I didn't see him."

"What did you do with the letter from those people who considered buying that land?"

"We left it there, on the table," Dodie replied.

Henry chuckled. "John could have given Luke that letter then and there and told him what the facts were. Of course, Luke's problem is that there are not many known suspects. He has to cover everybody close to the judge and that means every one of us."

Midge dropped her knitting and gave a little squeal. "That's a dreadful thing to say! It was somebody we don't know about who shot the judge. Everybody says that he made some money during those old days of rum-running. There must have been somebody he quarreled with and somebody who wanted to get even with him."

Henry said, "The trouble with that is that it was such a long time ago. The judge was highly respectable"—there was a dry note in the word—"during the last twenty years of his life. I doubt if he kept up any of those old connections. In fact, I imagine he did everything possible to cut them off. Besides, that whole setup for rum-running was scattered to the winds long ago. But it would be a very desirable answer," he said with a wistful sigh.

Very desirable indeed, Cayce thought, as he walked home. But he didn't think it a likely answer.

He wished he had been able to persuade Dodie to tell him what she had remembered of the evening the judge was murdered. It was clear only that she was unsure of its significance, not of the fact itself. It was also clear that whatever it was, it was very small. He was uneasy, for Dodie just might

112

take it into her head to explore it herself; he debated telling the sheriff of it but dismissed that at once; Dodie would not tell him, or the sheriff or anybody, until she was ready to tell, and that might be never. Yet she had looked frightened.

He thought of the evening just past, himself back again with Henry and Dodie and Midge as if he'd never been away, and of the revelation it had brought him. Yet his love for Dodie was so deeply a part of him that there was nothing surprising, nothing amazing about it. The only surprising thing was his belated discovery.

He wondered how long he had been in love with her. He thought for a long time about that, pausing to lean against a gatepost and smoke, and at last came to the by no means new or unique conclusion that there was no way to define, or describe, or mark the boundaries of love. There it was, like measles, except it lasted longer. Some of the clouds parted a little so he could see a few stars, and looking up at them, it seemed to him that some of the old poets were quite right when they swore their love by the stars that lasted forever.

The trouble was that he had always simply accepted Dodie, taken her enduring loyalty for granted, never until that night recognizing her place in his life. The trouble was, too, that he could see Dodie's point of view; he had deluded himself, reaching for Midge instead of his real lodestar, Dodie.

The scudding clouds left a patch of the sky very clear and the stars very bright. In the winter months, very clear, bright stars could mean a frost. The young trees were banked then, sometimes in a hurry, all the grove men working swiftly when the weather bureau gave warning of frost earlier than anybody expected it. But only the young trees needed banking; smudge pots were brought out for the older trees. He remembered the eerie, fiery glow above the smudge pots, which were placed strategically through the groves and sent out clouds of warming smoke.

The restoration of Blanchards had already taken on a deeper significance; although he wondered if in fact, all along, Dodie had been as ineradicably a part of Blanchards as she was of his own heart.

She hadn't listened to him; she wouldn't let him tell her how he felt. He was uneasy, without any real cause, about John. Yet when he put out his cigarette and strolled on slowly, toward the house, he whistled softly and happily.

Of course, there was the dangerous entanglement of the judge's murder from which he had to extricate himself, but just then everything seemed possible, nothing too difficult or too dangerous.

He even felt amused, thinking of Henry and his theories; Henry always had theories. If he decided that Midge and Dodie, daughters of a rich man as Henry must be, should do the household chores, then that's what they did. Henry had always expected and received obedience. He was kind, intelligent and, in a way, ruthless.

Suddenly, from nowhere really, it struck Cayce that murder required either an unstable or a peculiarly stable mind. If Henry, for instance, had decided that the judge should be murdered, he might have accomplished just that, efficiently and without remorse.

He rejected the errant reflection almost with horror. Henry was too smart to murder anybody. Even if—*even if he loved Cayce and loved justice and knew that the only way which would permit Cayce's return to his own land was by murder . . . No, no, he thought; Henry wouldn't have shot the judge!*

Besides Henry couldn't walk, he was tied to his wheel chair. But the wheel chair had made no lasting marks on the springy, tough lawn. So it would have made no lasting marks on the wiry crab grass that covered the lake path.

He stopped again, his hands thrust in his pockets, stunned at the irresistible course of his own thoughts. He felt as if he ought to go back and apologize to Henry. Henry had been almost like a father to him.

John had said something about that—"You're like a son to me," wasn't that it?

Like a runaway horse that ugly conjecture plunged on. John, too, wanted him to return to Blanchards.

He shook his head impatiently; he lighted another cigarette and noted the unsteadiness of his hands. Was there a spreading evil of murder, which like a noxious vine caught up and strangled everything within its reach, reason and knowledge and affection—so he could and did consider whether or not Henry—whether or not John—could have murdered the judge?

All right then, he thought; face it; root out those ugly tendrils of suspicion by cold, clear logic.

And there was no logic in such a hypothesis. A desire on the part of Henry—or of John—to restore to Cayce his rights and his land was simply not a motive for murder. A motive for murder had to be far stronger than that; it had to be direct and terribly urgent. Henry had said there were not many motives for murder: in the final analysis there were only the motives of money, fear and hatred.

All of them were, they must be, deeply personal—and he

thought again, terribly urgent. There wasn't anything really which, by the wildest stretch of the imagination, could be called a generous, an altruistic motive for murder.

He felt better then—a little ashamed, but better. As if leaving a dark and crawling enemy behind him, he walked on briskly now toward the house. When he came out of the driveway the clouds had again swept all across the night sky, covering the patch of clear stars. There was a light though in the house, his home—Dodie's home, sometime, he hoped—sometime.

He was in love with his wife! That was the legal truth of it. Except she wasn't really his wife—not yet.

He went into the house, and the light from the hall made a path into the living room, showing the familiar faded chintzes and the old rosewood piano. The table in the hall always held an enormous vase of flowers; there were great loops of wisteria in it that night, fragrant and sweet. No one was about; he went quietly upstairs.

Morning was clear with the sun streaking in golden rays across the treetops, burning away the blue-gray haze of the night. The lake was flat and peaceful, lightly touched with rose and gold. Near at hand the flowers were brilliant red and deep pink. It did not seem possible that a land of such fertile greens and luxuriant color could emerge from the darkness of the night. It was as if in the daytime the jungle conceded to man and all of man's labors, but in the nighttime took back her own.

Cayce was out of the house before anyone was stirring, planning work for the day. There was always the hard and constant routine: disc, harrow, fertilize, water, spray—disc, harrow, fertilize, water, spray. He wished he were three men. After he gave the two grove men their orders for the day he went to work himself among the neglected young trees; from what he now knew of the groves there would be many trees to be replaced.

The south grove was the largest tract and it was the oldest section of grove land at Blanchards too. It had been started at a time when orange trees grew high and thick, making picking difficult, making all the work of tending the grove more difficult. In recent years the trees were grown smaller, easier to reach, easier to care for, and bore heavy fruit.

Some of the trees in the south grove could be budded; he'd have to get hold of somebody who knew how to bud them, wrap them in their complicated bandages, and see that their life of rich production was renewed.

He was dragging out a sack of fertilizer when Sam Williams came around the end of the tool shed. Sam looked spruce and unwrinkled in a light gray suit and white shirt and he was very cheerful. "Give you a hand with that, Cayce," he said, and heaved up one end and helped Cayce edge the heavy sack into a wheelbarrow.

"Thanks, Sam. I need your help. The grove records—well, I guess everything is in a mess. I've got a little money saved. Not much, but enough to meet the payroll for a few weeks. After that . . ."

As they walked to the house he told Sam of what he had found, but Sam was still not prepared for the cluttered disorder. He gave Cayce a horrified look, took off his coat and arranged it neatly over a chair. "This is a job," he said, in what struck Cayce as wild understatement.

Blanche opened the door, looked at Sam seated at the desk in surprise, said, "Good morning, Sam," and turned to Cayce. "I wanted to remind you that the services for the judge are this afternoon at three."

"Is there anything you want me to do, Aunt Blanche?"

"Oh no, thanks," she said vaguely. "All the arrangements are made. What are you doing, Sam?"

Cayce replied, "I asked Sam to straighten out the grove and financial records. He's an accountant, you know."

"Oh," she said. "Well, I have to go to Tampa. Dodie said she would take me. Roddy's gone an hour ago. He'll be back, though, for the services. Be sure you're ready to go by three, Cayce. . . . There's Dodie's car now."

He heard the car stop in the circle. He said, "I'll see you at lunch, Sam," and went out with Blanche. Again she wore the black, simple dress which made her look different somehow, younger and more vital and energetic.

Dodie, too, wore a dress instead of her usual blue jeans or shorts. She said, "Good morning," and smiled politely and distantly. Her eyes looked as blue as the sky but there were faint, little shadows under them. "I telephoned to John this morning, Cayce. Nobody answered."

"What's wrong?" Blanche asked, getting into the front seat beside Dodie. "You phoned twice about John last night."

He didn't want to alarm Blanche. Besides, certainly, there was no need to alarm anybody. He said, "We wanted to talk to John and couldn't find him." He glanced at Dodie. "I'll go over there. Don't worry about it."

After they had gone he walked across the lawn to the path through the east grove.

It was growing very hot. They needed not just a shower but some good soaking rains. Cayce knew now that some of

116

the brownish spots on what had once been an emerald green lawn were due to the dry season. Usually in Florida there was all the rain anybody could want and, besides, the land was honeycombed by subterranean streams of water, always replenished and full. And there was the rainy season when, day after day, heavy, strong showers soaked into the land. Water was never a real problem in Florida but nevertheless it had been a comparatively dry season. All those dark and hidden streams needed replenishment.

He came out of the grove. The lights were still burning in John's cottage, looking weak and sickly in contrast to the brilliant, sparkling lake. John's car was still there. He went down to the landing platform and John's boat was still there.

But John was not in the cottage, he was nowhere around it, and nothing in the cottage had been changed. The empty glass still stood on the kitchen table. The end of Dodie's cigarette, showing a tiny pink stain of lipstick, still lay in the ash tray. There were dead insects, little clouds of them, on the table beneath the lamp.

But John was not there, and had obviously not been there. He debated for a moment. Then he went to the telephone and called the sheriff. The sheriff listened thoughtfully.

"You say he wasn't there last night?" he asked.

"No, but somebody was here. He left as we came. Dodie thought it was Zack."

There was a long pause. Then Luke said, "Stay there, will you? Don't touch anything. I'll be along in a few minutes."

As he put down the phone Cayce felt, rather oddly, that he had cut himself off from the bright sunlit world outside the heavy shadowy growth around John's cottage. Because the light looked sickly and strange and he didn't like the little heaps of insects which had worn out their short lives around those burning lights during the long night just passed, he flicked a switch, turning out the lights. Instantly, though, the porch fell into such green and shadowy gloom that he turned on the light again and went down to the little boat landing.

The narrow path through the bamboos was hot; there was not a breath of air. The boat landing was small—merely short strips of planking held in place by four great timbers, weather-beaten and silvery. John's boat moved sluggishly in the slight ebb and flow of the lake. The bamboos cast a shadow now over the landing. Later, when the sun was at its height, there would be no shadow at all. The oars of John's boat were still damp; they would dry when the sun reached them.

He thought of Dodie and the dark, faint shadow under her

117

eyes. Had she lain awake all night trying to discover what, if anything, that small memory which had returned to her meant? He couldn't rush Dodie; he had to wait. He heard Luke's car thudding jerkily along the bumpy road behind the cottage and went to meet him.

"John hasn't turned up yet?"

Cayce shook his head. Luke took off his hat and wiped his hot face. "Funny," he said. "I'm only a county sheriff, of course. Not up to all these scientific police doings. But they do say that one of the hardest things to do is to keep a murder witness safe."

The uneasiness that had come out of the blackness and stillness of the previous night returned, tugging at Cayce's nerves. The sheriff said, "Not that I think anything's happened to John. I mean, such as murder. But he did find the judge. Maybe he told me everything he knew or saw, and maybe he didn't. If he didn't, then whoever murdered the judge knew it . . ." He stopped and gave Cayce a queer, long look. "I'm not saying John's been murdered. I'll take a look inside the house."

SEVENTEEN

It didn't take long.

"His car is here," Luke said, sitting down in one of the reed chairs with a sigh. "Boat is here. You say the oars were wet last night. You mean wet, or just damp?"

"Wet. He'd used the boat—sometime after the inquest."

"He'd used it," Luke said somberly, "or somebody else used it."

The letter from the man who had inquired about buying the land lay on the table; he gave it to Luke, who read it carefully.

"John could have let me know about that when I questioned him. But I guess it doesn't matter. Did the judge ask you whether or not you'd sell this piece of land?"

"No."

"Maybe that's why the judge sent for you."

"I doubt it. That letter is dated nearly two months ago."

Luke said suddenly, "Turn off those lights, will you? Can't stand seeing all those dead bugs around."

Cayce flicked the switch again. Luke said, "Clothes still here. Razor still here. Maybe he took something with him— I wouldn't know whether or not all his clothes are here. He could always buy another razor." He went to the screen and looked out across the lake. "The trouble is," he said, "it would be so easy to get rid of anybody around here." He nodded vaguely toward the lake. "All that—out there. Swamplands in behind, running all the way to the Burke place. Man could lie out there sinking into the swamp, covered with vines and vegetation—nobody'd ever find so much as his bones."

"Don't!" Cayce said.

Luke's eyes pinned him with a steely sharpness. "You've grown up, Cayce. Steadier. You quarreled plenty with the judge when you were a kid, but you never did anything about it. Now—I don't know. I don't accuse you of murder. But I think you *could* have murdered the judge if you'd made up your mind that you had to. On the other hand I don't think you'd—get rid of John," Luke said obliquely. "Come on, let's get out of this place."

Once out in the cleared space, though, Luke examined John's car minutely. "Looks like John came home from the inquest, had himself a drink or two, took his boat out sometime later, brought it back and—disappeared." He got into his car and started the engine. "Guess I'll have to talk to Zack."

"Luke, what about those footprints? The mold you took yesterday? Have you had a report?"

"Oh, sure. About what I expected. Nothing much. If Dodie hadn't brushed over those footprints near the path we might have had something to identify. As it is, almost anybody could have made that one footprint. Seems a little wide to be a woman's footprint, but that's about all anybody can say."

"Does the scar on it match up with the scar on my foot?"

"Well—no," Luke said.

"Then somebody did make that, faked it. That's proof of it!"

"There's no proof of anything." Luke glanced back at the low, vine-draped cottage and said unexpectedly, "Something about that place I don't like. I'd have said I didn't have any nerves but . . ." He sighed and clapped his hat back on his head. "See you later, Cayce."

Cayce watched as the sheriff's car rounded a clump of stark, black oaks laden with Spanish moss, and vanished behind them. He went back then along the grove path.

Shortly before three he got out the judge's car and took Blanche to Val Roja and the little white church with its vines, its great hedges of scarlet blooming hibiscus and its white steeple, pointing upward. There was already a circle of auto-

119

mobiles parked before the church and around the corner.

Roddy was waiting for them and came with sober and grave demeanor to assist his mother from the car. Both of them, Cayce thought, half-amused and half-touched, were mourning with a certain ostentation, as if some of the influence of the Spanish Velidas had rubbed off on them. Blanche had worn her black dress and smart, little black hat; she now, covertly before she got out of the car, adjusted a thick black veil over her hat. It was almost the length of her skirt, and was so thick that her pale features were obscured. It must have been stifling on so warm a day. Cayce knew dimly that Spanish mourning customs were rigid and long; he wondered if Blanche would wear unrelieved black for a year. Roddy was wearing black, too; Cayce wondered where he had got the heavy black suit which did not fit Roddy's tall, thin body; perhaps he'd borrowed it from a Velidas cousin.

Strangely, during the services, which were very short, he began to think of the judge not with sorrow or grief but with a kind of pity. He wouldn't have wanted him to die like that, and the judge had never had what he really wanted in life, which was power and money. The substitutes he had grasped from Blanchards—money and his limited power over Roddy and Blanche and Cayce, until Cayce had escaped him. But Cayce doubted whether the judge had ever been a happy man.

The little minister was having a hard time; he said very little of the judge himself, and his honest blue eyes were troubled.

Dodie and Midge sat near them; Midge sat with her eyes cast down sedately; Dodie stared straight ahead and Cayce did not think she was listening. The church was full of flowers and their fragrance was heavy and strangely exotic.

When it was over and he went out, following Blanche and Roddy, Cayce saw that the little church was so full that people were standing at the back. He knew that he was under scrutiny; how many of them thought that he was responsible for the judge's death?

Cayce drove the car to the small, old cemetery which was very peaceful; a large stone with CLARY carved deeply upon it marked his father's and mother's graves. Huge old oak trees dripping with Spanish moss gave a quiet shade. Someone had seen to it that the Clary lot was weeded and planted with flowers; that should have been his task, Cayce thought. He had failed in many ways to keep a kind of compact with his father and with a self-estimate of his own character. He couldn't blame the judge for his own failures.

On the way home, when they were safely distant from other automobiles streaming from the cemetery, Blanche sighed and removed her veil. The sheriff's car stood in the circle before the house, and the sheriff himself was sitting on the steps of the porch, looking very fine in his fresh, white linen suit and white Panama hat. Obviously he had attended the services. He spoke to Blanche, his hat in his hand. Then he turned to Cayce. "I want to talk to you, Cayce."

Again they walked around the house to the side entrance and into the study. Sam had gone, probably with Judith to the church. The room was dusky and hot; the desk looked inordinately neat, as if Sam had carefully put every paper in the safe or the desk, every pencil in the holder, emptied every ash tray. The sheriff said, "It was a nice service. Minister had kind of a hard time thinking up fine things about the judge. Fact is . . . ." Luke thought for a moment. "I guess he stuck to religion. And a good thing."

"Have you found John?"

"No. He wasn't at the church. He's not been in his office in Tampa; the elevator man doesn't remember seeing him for two or three days. Of course, his office is only on the second floor and John could have walked upstairs, without being seen by anybody. But I got the keys from the building manager and went in. Dusty. Doesn't look as if he's been there."

"Luke, where is he?"

The sheriff leaned back, took up a magazine and fanned himself with it. "As I see it, there are three possibilities." He paused, flapping the magazine and thinking. Cayce's city clothes were stickily hot; he pulled off his jacket. Luke said, "You see, John thought an awful lot of your father. Wouldn't have come here to live if he hadn't. He thought a lot of you, Cayce."

"I know that."

"You asked him to act as your lawyer. So it does seem queer for John to disappear like this. I mean, seems as if he'd stick to you and try to help."

Cayce's throat was suddenly very dry.

Luke looked at him. "Now I'm not saying anybody murdered him. I said there were three possibilities, and, of course, murder is one of them. But John just might have got some screwball notion."

"What do you mean?"

"I think you know what I mean. Maybe he got some notion that he would disappear, so all of us would think he'd killed the judge and was scared and running. He'd stay away just long enough to give you some time to get things straight-

121

ened out. If he could give the police the idea that he had shot the judge, we'd have to look for him. That would take the heat off you for a while. Meantime, maybe some evidence would come up that would nail the murderer. It doesn't make sense to me. But it might make sense to John."

Knowing John, it did make sense. "I suppose that letter about the land suggested that to you."

"When anybody starts trying to protect anybody else in a murder case they're asking for trouble."

Could he possibly have guessed that if Cayce was right in his surmise Dodie was trying to do exactly that? Cayce said, "I'm not trying to protect anybody but Cayce Clary. What's the second possibility?"

"Oh," Luke said in a weary voice, "drunk."

There was a long pause. The shadows of the azaleas lay heavy in the room. Cayce snapped on the light with its glowing green shade, and the crystal orange instantly picked up delicate lights amid its fragile green-enameled leaves and gold tracing. "Do you think that's it?"

"Well, I've never known him to disappear like this. Of course, he may be in Tampa somewhere. The police there are keeping an eye out for him. He didn't leave by plane and so far as we know now he didn't leave by train, but that's kind of hard to check. And then, he could have got a lift into Tampa or into Suncas City." Luke sighed and rubbed his big nose with irritated vigor. "I do wish, though, he had taken his car. Somehow I just can't see him starting out on foot somewhere last night. But if he'd been anywhere around he'd have turned up at the funeral."

Cayce moved a blotter out of its orderly alignment on the desk, and back again. "What's the third possibility?"

"Maybe I should have put that first. That's obvious. Suppose he really did murder the judge."

"Why?"

"If I knew everything," Luke snapped irritably, "I could answer that and a lot of other things. . . . Zack says he wasn't at the cottage last night. Says he was looking for a job. Drove over to Suncas City to see a grove man there, but didn't find him. It's nothing that can be substantiated."

"Luke, suppose Zack shot the judge. He was here on the place at the time the judge was shot. And there might have been some reason for it."

"Why would he kill the judge and risk being fired by you?"

"He thought I would need him. He didn't expect me to fire him."

"Maybe you acted kind of quick. Zack isn't a bad grove

122

man. Your groves did all right till a few years ago." There was a strong suggestion of knowledge in Luke's manner.

"You know what the judge did with the money?"

Luke nodded. "Henry Howard told me. Said he thought I ought to know. He said, too, that you had got hold of the deed and that Miss Blanche, as the survivor, has a life tenancy here. What are you going to do about that?"

"I don't know." Cayce hesitated, and then went on. "Roddy offered to settle with me. Split the money the judge salted away and say no more about it."

Luke looked very shrewd. "What did he want for that?"

"Silence, I suppose. He said that I was likely to need money —for a good trial lawyer."

Luke thought for a moment, then he leaned back again in the maroon chair. "I guess I'll have a little talk with Roddy. Ask him to come in here, Cayce. Without his mother."

Roddy came in promptly. He had changed from his heavy black, somehow foreign-looking suit into brown shorts and a cream-colored silk shirt.

"Did you try to make a deal with Cayce?" the sheriff asked bluntly.

"A deal?" Roddy said in a tone of surprise. He sat down at the desk and picked up the crystal orange and turned it in his fingers, watching the glancing lights. "I don't know what you're talking about," he said pleasantly.

EIGHTEEN

It was no more and no less than Cayce might have expected. The sheriff said in a quiet way, but his eyes were very steely, "How long have you known that Miss Blanche had a life tenancy at Blanchards—if the judge predeceased her?"

The orange stopped turning for a second. Then Roddy said, "Only after the judge was killed."

Cayce said, "You told me that you had known that for years."

This time Roddy merely lifted his eyebrows, smiled and did not so much as utter a further denial.

"When did you find out about it?" the sheriff asked.

Again there was the slightest hesitation in Roddy's reply. Then he said with an effective frankness, "I got the deed out of the safe the night the judge died."

"Now why did you do that?"

"Because the judge had been killed." Roddy shrugged.

123

"Cayce had been here that afternoon. If he'd gone so far as to murder the judge he would not stick at taking anything that belonged to—to my mother. I didn't know that the life tenancy clause in the deed was written just like that, but I thought I ought to take a look in the safe and see that anything that belonged to my mother was taken care of. She wouldn't have thought of such a thing."

"You knew how to open the safe?"

"Of course," Roddy said smoothly. "Uncle Cayce showed me the combination. I often helped him with this and that. He gave me a key to the desk here, too."

Again Cayce couldn't let it pass. "You told me that you had figured out the safe combination years ago. You said you got the judge's key and had a duplicate made."

Roddy smiled. "Now why would I do that when the judge had already given me both?"

Luke said, "What did you do with the deed?"

Again Roddy answered with apparent frankness. "I took it to Tampa and had a photostat made. Cayce could have destroyed it. My mother would then have had no provable claim. I had to protect my mother's interest."

The sheriff fumbled in a pocket of his linen coat. He was already beginning to look less dressed up, more like himself, for the white linen was becoming rumpled. He got out a battered package of cigarettes, eyed it, and said, as if addressing the cigarettes, "What does Miss Blanche think about all this?"

Roddy put the orange down on the desk. "This is my mother's home. It has been her home for a long time. Cayce's father very clearly expressed his wish for her to consider it her home all her life." He looked at Cayce. "And while we're talking of this, Cayce—what's Sam Williams doing in this house?"

Ten years ago, even a week ago, Roddy's air of authority alone would have roused Cayce. Now, he thought only, what's Roddy getting at? "I employed Sam to get the grove books in order."

"*You* employed him," Roddy said. "Why didn't you consult my mother?"

"Sam is a certified public accountant," Cayce replied mildly. "We need him."

"All right," Roddy said. There was a deep, cold flash in his eyes. "I didn't want to say this, Sheriff. I wouldn't want to get Sam into trouble. I don't think he shot the judge. But the fact is . . ."

Cayce saw then what he was getting at. He cut in swiftly, "The judge asked Sam to do his taxes. He offered him a thousand dollars to make inaccurate statements. Sam wouldn't do it."

Roddy said, "You weren't here, Cayce. I was. It happened in this room. Sam defied the judge. The judge said some things to Sam; you'd call them threats. He said he'd see to it that Sam didn't get another job around Tampa. Sam said he didn't want work like the judge's and the judge—before I could stop him, he slapped Sam." Roddy sat back in the chair, composed and cool, and waited.

Nobody spoke. Was he lying again? A very convincing lie was one that was composed of a little truth and a large leaven of likelihood. It would have been like the judge to strike Sam, remembering only the boy, a nephew of the cook next door, who had fished and played with the other children, and forgetting that he was now a man.

Luke said finally, "That was a bad thing to do. Sam is a fine boy. He didn't tell me anything about this."

"Naturally not," Roddy said. "And mind you, I'm not accusing Sam of shooting the judge. But I don't want him around here."

"You'll have to get used to it," Cayce said. "Sam is going to get all this in order and it's going to take a long time. . . ."

Blanche in the doorway said, "Why, Sheriff! I thought you had gone. Will you have something cool to drink?"

Luke struggled to his feet. Roddy sprang up in a single graceful motion. Cayce stared at Blanche. He was all wrong about Spanish mourning customs rubbing off on Blanche. She was wearing a thin, simple, green dress with a tiny figure in white stitched in around the neck and around the sleeves, which even Cayce knew was expensive and smart. Her red hair was smooth and shiny, without a hair out of place. She wore a tiny string of pearls at her throat and high-heeled dark-green linen slippers. She was chic, elegant as Roddy. Cayce thought with stunned surprise, why, she must have been a beauty one time.

That was the reason for her trips to Tampa; she had been buying clothes! No more dowdy, frilly, sagging, old-fashioned dresses for Blanche.

The sheriff seemed a little stunned, too, for he was looking at Blanche as if he had never seen her before in his life. He said finally that, no, he wouldn't have a drink just now, but he'd like to ask her a few questions.

Blanche looked at the sheriff tranquilly. "Yes, Sheriff?"

"How long have you known that you shared a life tenancy in Blanchards with the judge, Miss Blanche?"

"What?"

Roddy said quickly, "Your life tenancy, Mother. You know, with the judge. The survivor retains the life tenancy."

"But I—I didn't know it. Is that true?"

For a moment no one replied. The sheriff looked deeply thoughtful. Roddy eyed the little crystal orange and two small scarlet patches crept up over his high cheekbones. Blanche turned to Cayce. "Is that true, Cayce?"

"Yes, Blanche. It's written in the deed."

She thought for a moment, her dark eyes a deep and cloudy brown. Then she said, "Did you know this, Cayce?"

"No, Aunt Blanche."

She turned to Roddy. "Did you know it?"

"Not—until the night after the judge was killed."

"But that—does that mean . . ." Blanche put her hand on Cayce's arm. "I asked you when you wanted me to leave, and you said that it was my home. Is that why?"

"I didn't know about the deed then."

"Oh," Blanche said. "Oh." She turned to the sheriff. "This place belongs to Cayce. Nobody can make me stay here and take any more money from him. That may be in the deed but nobody can force me to accept it." She smiled at the sheriff politely, said good night and walked out of the room.

The sheriff rose, took a long breath, said in an absent and wistful way something that sounded like "watermelons," opened the screened door and went out. Roddy put down the crystal orange with a thud. "My mother did not know of her name in the deed. She's telling you the truth. I hope you do her the respect to believe it."

And instantly Blanche's statement took on a dubious quality. Cayce had believed her implicitly when she spoke; now he questioned it. That was because he had to question anything Roddy said.

Could she have lived in that house all those years and not have known the exact terms of the deed? Wouldn't his father have discussed it with her, as certainly as he must have discussed it with the judge? So if Blanche had lied, then why?

Because, with the judge dead, Blanche was sole arbiter of Blanchards and Roddy was her son. In that sense it was to Roddy's advantage and to Blanche's advantage to kill the judge.

There were arguments against that, cogent arguments. Blanche had never had much to say about the place; she hadn't seemed interested in it; she hadn't even cared about keeping up the flower gardens, renewing the faded chintzes, doing anything which would imply affection or pride or sense of ownership.

Again Cayce felt baffled and frustrated; it was as if Blanche had walked through life amid veils, like the long black veil she had worn that afternoon.

Cayce said abruptly, "When did you last see John?"

There was a startled flash in Roddy's dark eyes. "John? Why?"

"He seems to have disappeared."

"What do you mean, disappeared?"

"He's not at his house. His car is there and his boat is there."

Roddy eyed him for a moment, his dark eyes guarded; yet Cayce could feel a swift activity behind them.

"Do the police know about it?"

"Yes. They're trying to find him."

"I noticed he wasn't at the funeral," Roddy said slowly, and Cayce wondered how in the world he had managed to see that, while keeping his gaze decorously bent downward all the time. "That would be very convenient for you, wouldn't it? John has disappeared. Therefore he murdered the judge and got away. There's your solution all fixed for you. John gets blamed, indicted in absentia, so to speak, for the murder. He goes off to live quietly in some place you've agreed upon. You send him the money to keep him going. So now he's a hero, taking the blame, but getting paid and paid well for doing it. And all the time basking in the thought that he has saved his friend's son. Isn't that the way it is?"

"No, that's not the way it is."

"It's what the police will think. So you'll be well out of an arrest on a murder charge and—if the way people felt at the inquest yesterday is an indication, a conviction for murder."

"It take a jury to convict anybody."

"Juries are people," Roddy observed incontrovertibly and walked with lazy arrogance out of the room.

He'd won that round, Cayce thought wryly. But there was a troubling element of credibility in the conclusion to which Roddy had leaped so promptly. Everybody knew of John's friendship with Cayce's father; wouldn't many people believe that John had quietly taken the rap for Cayce?

One thing was clear; the nebulous business of the exact definition of that deed had to be cleared up as soon as possible and before Cayce's money ran out. Hadn't John mentioned another lawyer? Yes; the name returned to him; Charles Penn is your man, remember it, John had said. For an instant a question flickered across Cayce's mind; had John said that so definitely, so promptly, because even then he intended to

127

disappear and he wanted to make sure that Cayce went to a good lawyer? Certainly John had mentioned Charles Penn's name very shortly after that odd and cunning look had flashed into his face.

Yet if John had disappeared voluntarily, sometime, somewhere, they would find him. John would have known that. But again Cayce remembered the look of neatness and order in John's cottage. There was nothing to suggest a hurried packing and an intentional departure. He wondered if it would be possible to drag the lake; he knew that only by chance could a search of the swamplands be either complete or successful.

He was thankful when Belle called him to dinner. It was still very hot; the air in the dining room was stifling. Blanche did most of the talking, and Cayce could not keep his eyes from that slender, youthfully erect figure in its smart, green dress. He thought oddly it was as if he were watching a butterfly emerge from its dull, gray and immobile cocoon. He wondered when the wings would rise and gain strength. That was fanciful; this was only Aunt Blanche, who was saying that the church had been full; somehow she had seen everything through that thick veil. She knew that the organist had touched the wrong stop by mistake and for a second the vox humana had quavered through the little church. "Anna was so embarrassed," she said. "And, by the way, the wreath the Suncas City Club sent was wilted. I think the committee ought to speak to the florist. . . . John wasn't there." She looked at Cayce. "I saw—well, it looked like state troopers at his cottage. Where is John?"

Blanche always saw and heard more than anyone suspected. Cayce said, "He's—gone. Nobody knows where."

There was a flash of something—alarm?—in her changeable dark eyes. "But surely he wouldn't leave, just now! Without telling anybody!"

Roddy said softly, "Do you think he shot the judge, Mother?"

Blanche's eyelids lowered. "Why, how silly! Don't say things like that, Roddy. . . . It's so warm in here. If you've finished dinner . . ."

Cayce drew out her chair. She said vaguely, "Thank you," and walked out of the room.

Roddy eyed Cayce. "John wouldn't have come to the services even if he'd been here."

"Why not?"

Roddy shrugged. "John asked too many questions about the management of the groves. The judge told John he drank too much and a man with his history wasn't welcome here, and he'd better shut up and stay away."

"How do you know that?"

Roddy gave him a smiling glance in which there was a touch of scorn. "I've got ears."

Was Roddy telling him the truth? Cayce said slowly, "When did that happen?"

"Oh—they'd not been getting along for some time. That particular little row happened only a few weeks ago. They were in the study. I chanced to stroll along the path outside the study door."

It might be the truth, Cayce thought; it was easy to believe that anybody, even John, would quarrel with the judge—especially if John had asked too many and too inconvenient questions about what the judge was doing with the money from the groves. And he had questioned him, as Henry had done, and frankly and with a touch of pride had admitted it. Cayce said slowly, "What did the judge mean by saying a man with John's history?"

"That's clear enough, I should think. John is no financial genius. And he is a drunk. He had no right to inquire into the judge's affairs." His eyes narrowed, watching Cayce, with a little smiling gleam. "I wonder if I ought to tell the sheriff about that."

"Let's get this straight," Cayce said, answering the triumphant little smile rather than Roddy's words. "Do you mean you think John might even have killed the judge because the judge told him . . ."

"He told him to mind his own business," Roddy broke in swiftly. "And don't forget. John said he found the judge. He said he didn't see any other boat or anybody around. He said he didn't hear the shot. And John was always talking about you, saying you ought to come home. Maybe he 'found' the judge all right—after he'd shot him."

Cayce finished his coffee deliberately and rose. "You say I killed the judge. You suggest, very adroitly, that Sam killed him. Now you say John did it. Make up your mind, Roddy," he said and went out through the study and down to the fishing pier.

There were no lights in John's cottage. He hadn't expected to see lights—yet the utterly empty blackness added to his increasing apprehension. Surely if John were alive, he'd have returned by now.

He sat on the pier, dangling his legs above the water, smoking and thinking. There was a modicum of truth in Roddy's accusation of John; Cayce himself had considered whether or not John might have shot the judge in order to bring about Cayce's return. There was an important flaw in Roddy's reasoning, though: if John had shot the judge, would he have said so definitely that there had been no other boat on the lake and that he had seen no one, anywhere? Wouldn't he have made some effort to protect himself from the very arguments Roddy had seized upon?

Probably Roddy, in his heart, knew that too. Certainly Roddy was only interested in casting the seeds of suspicion indiscriminately, anywhere, so long as none of them fell upon Roddy himself.

Yet he didn't really believe that Roddy had killed the judge. He *had* rescued the judge from the lake when, if he'd wanted the judge to die, all he had to do was do nothing. And while the judge might have rebelled at Roddy's blackmailing activities, there was no evidence of it. It was conceivable that Roddy had, all along, planned to get his fingers on at least a part of the money the judge had milked from Blanchards, but killing the judge in that hope was altogether too uncertain a gamble for Roddy, or anybody, to take.

A flying little cloud of insects discovered him, swirled about his face, and drifted off above the lake. Again the night was secretive, controlled by the old, strong forces of the tropics and the jungle. He listened to the faint lap of water against the boats. How long would it take for a man's body to come to the surface? If it were weighted, if it were sucked down deeper and deeper into the muddy bottom, perhaps it would never be found.

He had to go to John's cottage again. Perhaps, just perhaps, John had returned and was sitting there in the dark, alone.

He found his way again along the grove path, the long way, instead of taking one of the two boats tied to the pier. Leaves thrust through the fetid darkness and brushed his face. At last he reached the cottage, turned on lights and called John. There was no answer, and everything—even the clouds of dead insects which still seemed to inhabit the silent cottage with their own whispering little lives—was the same.

He turned out the lights and went slowly back along the path, and then crossed the lawn, below the lights of his own house, and went into the lane between the great Australian pines. He had to see Dodie. By now perhaps she would be willing to share with him that memory which had seemed to her frightening and significant.

There were lights, too, in the Howard house. He had almost reached the terrace when he heard Dodie scream from somewhere in the deep blackness near the lake.

NINETEEN

He shouted, "Dodie—Dodie . . ." and ran toward the lake.

If there were any other sounds, the rustle of shrubbery or other running footsteps, Cayce couldn't have heard them above the pounding of his own heart. He came to the pool, a rectangle of lightness in the surrounding black, skirted it, his footsteps hard and quick on the concrete that ran around it, and headed for the boat landing.

"Dodie . . ." he called again, and stumbled over the boat landing and saw her, a white, dim figure. He caught her and took her in his arms and was half smothered by a thin, tough blackness that got between them.

He thrust away the clinging, black thing; it was some kind of thin, wispy material. He felt her face, her neck, her body. "I'm all right," she sobbed. "He was in the mangroves—he's gone. When you shouted he dropped it, and—oh, Cayce!"

He must search the mangroves. He must send out an alarm. But first he must get Dodie into the house. He half carried her, with Dodie clinging to him.

They had heard her scream from the house. Judith flung open the hall door and was already running down from the terrace, her flowered dressing gown flapping.

She didn't question. She didn't stop for anything. They got Dodie into the house and onto the sofa in the library. And Dodie, her hands at her throat, her eyes huge and terrified, cried, "He tried to choke me. He put something around my throat and pulled and—I screamed. I must have screamed . . ." Her eyes widened and fixed upon the thing Cayce carried in his hand.

He hadn't known that he had brought it with him. It was as if it had a willful, stubborn life of its own and clung to him. Judity said, *"It's a mourning veil!"*

It was a mourning veil, thick and black and tough. It was a veil such as Blanche had suddenly whipped out and pulled down over her face and arms, almost the length of her skirt. Its soft, black touch was revolting; Cayce flung it down as he would have flung down a huge, black spider.

Henry called from the top of the stairs, "What is it? Judith! Dodie!"

"He needs help down the stairs," Judith said and flashed out of the room.

Cayce thought of the mangroves, the great growths of shrubbery, the spreading wide acres of grove land which surrounded the place for hundreds of acres. Already whoever had been at the boat landing had had time to escape. He took up the telephone and told the operator he wanted the sheriff and to hurry. Luke answered sleepily. "Yes, hello—this is Sheriff Weller . . ."

"Luke, it's Cayce. I'm at the Howard place. Somebody tried to—to strangle Dodie. Just now. He was in the mangroves at the Howard boat landing."

"Phone the State Police. It'll save a little time while I get on some clothes."

Judith appeared again carrying dripping white towels in her capable hands. "Lie back there against the cushion, Dodie. Don't look like that. You're not hurt."

There was a gliding, smooth sound as Henry's wheel chair came into the room; he hadn't turned on the motor, he propelled it along with heavy sweeps of his arm. "Is she all right, Judith?"

Dodie answered. "Frightened," she said. "That's all."

"Where did it happen?"

"I went down to the boat landing. Oh, I know you told us not to go out of the house, but I wanted to see if there was a light in John's cottage, if he'd come back. I was standing there and—there was a kind of rustle in the mangroves. I couldn't see anything. I turned around and then—that—came over my head and around my throat." She looked at the black cloud on the floor.

The operator said in Cayce's ear, "I've got the police." A pleasant Southern voice said, "Yes? What's the trouble?"

Cayce explained concisely—the Howard place, near Val Roja. Attempted murder—he stopped there and thought with utter cold horror, attempted murder.

"Val Roja!" the easy voice quickened. "Why, that's where Judge Moore was murdered."

"He got away," Cayce said. "We can't search the place without help. . . ."

"We're on our way." The telephone clicked.

When he turned from the telephone Midge was standing in the doorway staring at the ugly little heap of black on the floor. She moved toward it slowly, her steps as precise as a dancer's and stooped to pick it up. She held it out so its long stifling length touched the floor. "Why, it's Miss Blanche's mourning veil!"

132

Henry's face was as white as marble; only his eyes blazed. "Do you know who it was, Dodie?"

Dodie's eyes, still huge and dark, went to her father's face, then away. "No. I knew somebody was there and then the veil came down over my face and around my throat and I screamed. I didn't hear Cayce coming. I didn't hear anything. But then Cayce was there, and all at once, whoever it was had gone. I knew that because the veil seemed to loosen around my throat."

"Cayce, did you see anybody down there?" Henry asked.

"No. He must have heard me coming. I ran along the concrete beside the pool. He had plenty of time to duck back into the mangroves."

"He?" Midge said, and eyed the veil that belonged to Blanche.

Henry leaned forward, his corded hands grasping the arms of his chair. "Think, Dodie, there must have been something that you recognized or remember."

She moved her head with its dark disheveled curls. "Nothing."

"Was it a man? Are you sure of that?"

"Yes—no, I'm not sure, really. There wasn't anything, not anything at all but a sound of someone near me and *that*." Her gaze touched the heap of black.

"Could it have been a woman?"

Dodie said, "You're thinking of Miss Blanche because that's her mourning veil. We all saw it this afternoon." She closed her eyes.

Henry said slowly, "Cayce—how did it happen that you came just then?"

Dodie's eyes flared open. "Don't speak to Cayce like that. Cayce wouldn't hurt me. He saved my life."

Cayce said, "I had gone over to see if John had got back. Then I wanted to talk to Dodie so I came over here. Just as I reached the end of the terrace I heard her scream."

"Dodie," Henry asked gently, "*why* do you suppose anybody would try to murder you?"

"I don't know." Dodie closed her eyes again.

Car lights flashed across the windows. Judith said, "It's the sheriff!" Her red and green flowered dressing gown swirled around her as she ran out of the room.

Luke came in panting; his face looked drawn and old and there was a faint stubble of gray beard on his chin. His manner with Dodie, however, was easy. "Throat all right now? No harm done?"

Dodie shook her head.

After a moment, he said, "I've got to talk to you now, Dodie, alone."

Alone with Luke meant alone; he was firm about it. He made even Henry leave the room and he closed the door after them.

In the hall, Judith asked Henry if he'd like some coffee and since Henry, sitting in his wheel chair, his hands gripping its arms, his head bent, did not seem to hear, Judith said that perhaps the sheriff wanted coffee, waked up in the middle of the night like that. She disappeared toward the kitchen. Midge sat on the lower steps of the stairs. There was a steady but muffled sound of voices from the library; Luke's heavy yet easy voice, questioning Dodie, and her murmurs for replies. Once Dodie's voice rose, "I tell you it *wasn't* . . ." They could not hear the rest of it.

But they did know it when Luke went to the telephone for they heard him say very loudly and clearly as one always spoke over the country line. "Miss Blanche, this is Luke Weller." They couldn't hear the rest of it but they knew that he was asking Blanche about her veil.

Cayce went past Henry's immobile figure and stood in the doorway to the terrace. There was one thing certain; the attack upon Dodie eliminated two people from that very short list of suspects—Midge and Henry. Neither of them would have hurt Dodie. And then he thought with a kind of horror, had he really in his heart suspected either Henry or Midge of killing the judge?

Luke opened the library door. "The State Police ought to be here soon," he said. "Come in here, Cayce."

Dodie was sitting up against the cushions holding a wet towel to her throat. Luke closed the door. "Dodie's told me the truth, Cayce. She says she told you how she came out of the house, just as the bombers went over, and went down to the boat landing—and then had a swim and got dressed again, and went to the fishing pier and found the judge. What I want to know is—has she told me—finally told me *all* the truth?"

She hadn't; Cayce was sure of that from the pleading look she gave him. He sat down beside her and took her hand. "Dodie, there's got to be a reason why somebody tried to kill you with that veil. You told me that you remembered—something, you wouldn't say what. Whatever it is, I think it's dangerous—to you. Tell me, Dodie. Tell Luke."

Her eyes wavered. Finally she sighed and gave up. "But it was so trivial. Nothing really. Only a boat. That is—really

134

just part of a boat, sticking out from behind the mangroves. I couldn't see all of it. But it was tied at the wrong side of the fishing pier."

TWENTY

"Whose boat?" Luke said harshly.

She glanced at him and away. "I could only see part of it. The mangroves got between. I only remembered, all at once, that it was there."

Cayce said slowly, "You said it was tied on the wrong side of the pier. You mean the judge usually tied his boats on the east side of the pier, and this boat was tied on the west side of the pier?"

"Yes. I thought the judge had been out on the lake and that's all. It was then I decided to go for a swim. When I came out of the cabaña I didn't go down to the landing. So I don't know whether or not the boat was still there."

"Well," Luke said slowly, "if it had been there when the judge was found, somebody would have seen it—Roddy or John or Zack. I inquired about boats but nobody saw a boat on the lake and the judge's boats by that time were tied to the east side of the pier. I saw that myself." He rubbed his nose worriedly. "The judge could have rowed out on the lake, brought his boat to the west side of the pier for some reason and tied it there. And then later returned it to the east side. . . . The point is—why didn't you want to tell anybody about it? What else did you see, Dodie?"

"I didn't see *anybody*! You can see the whole lake—or most of it, from the landing pier. You can't see the path on account of the mangroves. And in the cabaña you can see right straight across the lake, from the windows, but nothing else. When you're in the pool there's the cabaña and the mangroves between you and the lake and pier. So you see—I *couldn't* have seen anybody."

And suddenly Cayce thought there was still something that she was concealing. He didn't know why he thought that—perhaps because she was so quiet and still, watching the sheriff so warily.

The sheriff said, "Somebody tried to murder you, Dodie. The only reason for that must be because there's something you know. Did you tell anybody except Cayce that you came out of the house immediately after the bombers came over—or any of this?"

"No." She replied promptly this time and Cayce believed her.

The sheriff seemed uncertain. He eyed Dodie for a moment, started to speak, stopped and lights again swept across the windows. Two police cars came to a swift stop outside. "There's the police," the sheriff said. "Cayce, I spoke to your aunt about that veil. She said that she left it on a table in the hall, right beside the door, downstairs. She says the door was open. Anybody could have taken it. She says Roddy went out somewhere in his car, she doesn't know where, and she had gone to bed. So nobody was downstairs. And anybody could have looked through the windows of the living room, made sure that nobody was around—all he had to do then was open the door real quiet, and there was the veil. Nobody would have seen or heard it." He turned to Dodie. "Now then, Dodie, this is going to be tough. The police are going to ask you questions. They'll want to know why anybody would try to murder you." He went out of the room then, walking heavily and wearily as if he carried a burden on his shoulders.

They had a few seconds alone. Cayce said quickly, "Dodie, there's something you're not telling. I don't think it has anything to do with the boat. I think you did see somebody, somebody who had every right to be around, somebody who was so usual, somebody you were so accustomed to seeing that you didn't notice, not then. You didn't even think about it then. Who was it, Dodie?"

The police were already coming into the house. He heard Henry and the sheriff and an excited babble of questions.

Dodie merely looked at him and shook her head. "I didn't see anybody."

He caught her hand. "Well then, Dodie, you must have told somebody else about the boat. You must have tried to find out, inquire, settle some questions in your own mind. What was it?"

"I didn't tell anybody about it but you and the sheriff, Cayce. And I didn't ask anybody anything. I'm telling you the truth."

"She's in here," the sheriff said, opening the door.

A man in uniform came into the room. "I'm sorry about this, Miss Howard," he said. "We've got men searching the grounds. Can you give us any help? The smallest thing you can remember might help us to identify him."

Luke caught Cayce's attention and jerked his head in a commanding gesture toward the hall. Cayce obeyed reluctantly. Luke again closed the library door.

Midge was still sitting on the stairs. Henry, his eyes glowing like fiery coals in his white face, watched from his wheel chair.

There was a fragrant smell of coffee in the air. A silver tray with thin china cups and a huge kitchen coffeepot, which looked out of place on a silver tray and showed Judith's state of mind, stood on the table. Already there were lights out along the lake, the quick glancing rays of enormous flashlights. Somebody at a distance shouted a direction to somebody else.

The terrace door flung open and Roddy came in. "What happened? Mother told me somebody tried to strangle Dodie. She said it was her veil."

Midge explained. Henry lifted his sunken, yet fiery gaze, to Roddy. Roddy said, "But who did it? Who would hurt Dodie? Why?"

Cayce went out on the terrace, sat down on the balustrade and lighted a cigarette.

It was not likely that there were two murderers—or at least a murderer and a would-be murderer—within that narrow group of people, close to the judge and close to Dodie. So therefore, it was likely that whoever had murdered the judge had been, somehow, in spite of Dodie's denial, frightened. He was sure that she had not told the sheriff everything she knew—or at least everything she thought. In her anxiety, she must have sometime, somehow, let slip a word, an inquiry which warned the murderer. *It's hard to keep a witness safe*, the sheriff had said.

Blanche's veil was an ideal weapon in a dreadful way for it would show no fingerprints; it was tough and lethal and blinding to the victim. But Blanche certainly would not have used a weapon which led directly to her. Roddy would not have so involved his mother. Blanche, Roddy, Henry, even Midge—if he had to include everybody in the vicinity as a suspect—none of them would have attacked Dodie. There remained John and Zack. But John had disappeared before Dodie had remembered that boat, and whatever small but significant fact she was still concealing; she would have had no chance to talk to John. There was the likelihood, not proved but strong, that John had been murdered. He did not believe she had talked to Zack.

Perhaps that list of suspects was too short. There was always the possibility that there was an unknown enemy of the judge, somebody none of them knew about, but somebody who had a feeling only for his own safety, so strong and so urgent a need for self-preservation that he had to kill Dodie. The problem was how he could have guessed that Dodie was a danger to him.

And why would he have murdered John?

For the same reason, of course! John, too, in some way which he himself had not perceived might have possessed dangerous knowledge of the murder.

He still could not—or would not—accept John's murder as a fact.

The glancing flashlights were advancing in a kind of fan, having started with the mangrove thicket and the cabaña and the heavy growth around the lake and now spreading out. He wondered if, in that search, they would find John's body.

They did not find John's body; they did not find anyone. Toward dawn the search was extended to the Blanchards' grove, but by then it was a cursory search.

There were lights at Blanchards and Blanche was waiting when Luke came to talk to her again about her mourning veil. She hadn't heard anyone in the house; she hadn't heard the door open; no one had knocked or called to her. It developed that there was a space of about two hours to be accounted for—after Cayce had gone down to the pier and then at last to John's cottage, and Blanche herself had gone upstairs and Roddy had taken out his car and driven, he said, to Tampa.

"Why did you go to Tampa?" Luke asked.

Roddy shrugged. "I don't know. I just wanted to go somewhere. I went in a bar and had a drink." There was a scornful gleam in his eyes. "If you want an alibi for me, the bartender might remember. It was the Lotus bar."

Cayce couldn't remember anything called the Lotus bar but Luke nodded. "It's crowded. They might remember you and they might not."

Roddy said, "Are you trying to get alibis for everyone? I assure you I wouldn't have taken my mother's veil and tried to strangle Dodie. Why should I?"

After the sheriff had gone, Cayce sat for a while on the porch, smoking and watching the night darkness turn to gray. It was going to rain; he could smell it. Even Old Stinker, for the past few nights, had been curiously silent.

He sat up abruptly, his skin prickling. He knew alligators' habits. Attracted by the smell of blood, they found and seized upon prey but then took it away to some secluded inlet in the swamp and waited; they didn't like a fresh kill. It wouldn't have been necessary to put weights on a man's body and sink it into the lake until the muddy lake bottom sucked it down forever. Not on any lake where there were alligators.

The rain began, drumming faintly down on the groves, the lake, the house. Swiftly it became a heavy steady downpour.

If there had been any small marks in that mangrove thicket which the morning light might have disclosed, the rain would wash them away.

TWENTY-ONE

Cayce listened to the rain drumming down upon the house when he went back to the white kitchen to make coffee. He knew the thirsty land was soaking it up gratefully but at the moment it seemed like an enemy, a jungle force which had turned itself loose. He took the coffee into the study.

He awoke with his head on his arms on the desk and the green-shaded light burning. Every muscle was cramped and tired. It was still raining.

He crept upstairs for there was no sign from Roddy or Blanche, but by the time he came downstairs and into the kitchen the rain had stopped and sun was streaking through the remaining gray clouds.

When he went outside the grove men were already there, waiting for him, and somehow he knew that they had heard of the murderous attack the night before but they didn't question him.

Oddly that morning, for the first time since he returned, the groves and the entire place seemed to have taken a kind of new lease on life. Part of it, of course, was due to the lavish rain. But part of it was due to the fact that all at once, overnight it seemed, he could see some progress. The east grove and the west grove were now clean; the round of discing and harrowing showed almost immediate results. Again he started the men working in the largest tract, the south grove.

He'd have to look into the matter of spraying. The fruit was almost ready for picking. Probably the judge had already made a contract for the fruit; it was another item Cayce would have to investigate. It was almost noon when he returned to the house and Sam was at work in the study. "I heard about Dodie," Sam said. "Aunt Judith told me. She's all right this morning."

Cayce sat down. "Is there any other news?"

"Not that anybody over at Howards' knows about. I brought you the newspaper."

Cayce glanced at the headlines. "Murderer strikes again.

139

Daughter of prominent grove owner." He looked away. "Sam, Roddy says the judge—slapped you."

"Well, he did."

"He shouldn't have done that."

Sam understood what Cayce couldn't find words to say. He smiled. "Oh, that doesn't matter, Cayce. The judge still thought of me as a kid, you know. It's always hard for people to realize that children grow up." There was utter candor in Sam's face. "I wanted to hit him, I nearly did. I just caught myself in time and walked out. I guess," he said reflectively, "that made the judge even madder. You know how he was."

Oh yes, Cayce thought; I know. He got himself out of the chair and telephoned to Charles Penn.

Sam worked busily by his side while he talked. Charles Penn was at first a little reluctant. "Is this a criminal case?"

"I didn't kill the judge if you mean that. I just want you to get this deed straightened out, tell me where I stand, and what to do." He explained it quickly but exactly.

The lawyer's professional interest was aroused. "You'd better come in to see me and we'll thresh this thing out. It's unusual. But the groves are an income-producing property and I gather your father's intent was clear. Come in to see me."

Sam nodded with approval as Cayce put down the telephone. "That's the way to go at it, Cayce. You can't bulldoze it your way alone, you know. Do it legally and take your time."

"Have you seen any sort of contract for the sale of this year's fruit?"

"I haven't found anything for this year. Here are the records for last year. But I think this guy is a red dog dealer."

It was the local name for a purchaser who operated on a slim margin, who might not be too careful about the quality of the fruit he bought and thus was not likely to sell the fruit to a first-class canning or packing plant, or to a first-class shipper. Also, the red dog's checks were sometimes slow in arriving.

John's cottage drew Cayce again like a magnet. He went down through the muggy sticky heat to the fishing pier. Two policemen, in uniform, were on John's boat platform, two more were threshing through the swampy undergrowth beyond. It would be a futile search, Cayce thought dully and started for the Howard place. As he emerged from the Australian pines a car coming along the road stopped and waited. Zack sat at the wheel.

For a few seconds the sun again thrust through the morning's haze and burst out in a hot blaze upon Cayce as he walked across to Zack's car. "I wanted to talk to you, Zack."

The big man smiled. "I thought you would by now. You got a taste of what I can do in this county at the inquest, didn't you?"

"That isn't what I wanted to talk to you about."

"Oh, I guessed that, too. Ready to ask me to come back, are you? I figured it would take about three days. All right, I'll come. But you'll have to raise my salary."

Cayce looked at him thoughtfully. "Well, no," he said. "That's not what I wanted to talk to you about. What were you doing at John Tyron's cottage Wednesday night?"

"I don't know what you're talking about."

"Why did you go to the cottage?"

Zack looked at the wheel of his car. "Tried to get me into trouble, didn't you? Told the sheriff you'd seen me there. You didn't see me there. I didn't go there. Why would I want to see John Tyron? I've seen a lot of people the last few days. Out of a job, had to see a lot of people. But why would I go to see John Tyron? I'm a grove superintendent. He's got no work for me. And let me tell you . . ." Zack's confidence was returning. "Let me tell you, I've had some good offers, too. I wouldn't come back to work for you except I've been here so long I know the place. I've worked here since before you were born. You can't throw me out now."

Cayce eyed the big man's flabby body. "Want me to try it?"

Zack's little eyes flared open. "Now look here, Cayce, I'm not going to fight you!"

"Would you feel better if you had a gun?"

"So, you've accused me of murder! I didn't kill the judge and I don't know anything about John Tyron. If he's disappeared, it's because he shot the judge and knew they'd find out, and got away. They'll never find him."

Zack started up his engine with a roar. The sun glittered on his car until it swerved out of sight.

Zack was scared. And he *had* been at John's cottage. Cayce was sure of that. And if there had been any way of getting the truth out of Zack, Luke would have found it.

Cayce went back to the south grove and found that the small tractor had broken down. He took it to Val Roja. He had a sandwich and coffee at a little restaurant while the tractor was being repaired. He saw nobody he knew but he was conscious of the fact that everybody knew him, the men who worked on the tractor, the waitress in the restaurant, the men around the post office. Eyes followed him and a wave of silence which was broken excitedly when he was presumably out of earshot.

It was not entirely due to Zack that the whole county had already tried him and given the verdict of guilty. He *had* quarreled with the judge, he *had* run away, he *was* like a stranger, a foreigner, no longer one of them.

It was late in the afternoon by the time he got the tractor home again, so late that the grove men were leaving and the shadows of the trees lay low across the house and the lawn, now a brilliant emerald green from the rain. Sam had gone and the desk was neat and empty.

But Blanche was in the long comfortable living room, again wearing the smart green dress. Roddy wasn't home yet, she said, and there were drinks waiting for Cayce as soon as he had changed. "I'd like to talk to you then," she said, "but go ahead and get your shower first."

He could discover nothing from her attitude. Had Roddy persuaded her to exercise her right of life tenancy? Blanche would do anything for Roddy.

When he went downstairs again the sheriff was there. He wanted to talk to Cayce, he said.

They went outdoors and for lack of any other direction strolled past the sheriff's car, in the circle, and toward the fishing pier.

The sheriff looked gray with fatigue; he hadn't had any sleep at all the night before and obviously none that day. There was no news of John, he said; the state troopers had taken over and they had found neither John nor any clue to his disappearance. And, Luke said quietly, he had come to tell Cayce that he had to put him under arrest.

Cayce had half expected it for so long that there was no sense of shock. He said, as matter-of-factly as the sheriff had spoken, "But I didn't kill the judge, Luke."

"I don't like to arrest you, Cayce, and that's a fact. But I guess I've got to."

"You mean it's been four days and people are pushing you. Somebody's got to be arrested."

"Public opinion is a force. You can't hold out against it long. I was elected to enforce the law. I wouldn't send an innocent man to jail if I knew he was innocent. But a trial is a way of getting at the truth. It was the attack on Dodie last night that settled the thing. I've got to arrest you now."

TWENTY-TWO

"But I heard Dodie scream! I ran down there and found her . . ."

"Oh yes, you saved her. Folks around here don't think so."

"What do they think?" Cayce asked after a moment.

"Everybody around here knows that you and the Howard girls and Roddy were good friends. They don't know that Dodie found the judge long before John found him. They don't know what she did about those footprints near the path. They don't know Dodie's still married to you—I don't know that anybody even knows you two eloped. But what they do know is this. You saw Dodie and you saw John and talked to them, right after you had that quarrel with the judge. Then the judge was killed. John disappeared and—" he glanced out and around the lake, "there's plenty of ways of getting rid of a dead man around here if anybody really wants to and everybody knows that. Then last night somebody tried to strangle Dodie with Miss Blanche's veil. The plain fact is that people— and that includes the police—think Dodie and John may have been—maybe not witnesses but darn close to it. So they think you got rid of John and tried to get rid of Dodie. It all stacks up, you see. It makes sense to them. Logic."

A fish out in the lake leaped for some invisible insect and fell back into the water with a plop. Cayce watched the spreading circles until the last one rippled gently to the pier. He said then, "Can I talk to Dodie before you take me away?"

"She sticks to what she told me last night. I talked to her again today."

"I want to talk to her though," Cayce said stubbornly.

"You think if you tell her you're being arrested she may tell me something that'll help you out," Luke shook his head. "I don't think there's anything more to tell. I'm sorry, Cayce. I tried to give you a break, mainly because I didn't like the way the judge was letting Blanchards go to pieces. Your property and you were left in his care. It wasn't right but now I've got to arrest you. If I don't, the State Police will. I told them I would do it myself."

Cayce said slowly, "There are a few things I'd like to do."

"What?" Luke eyed another leaping fish wistfully, as if he wanted a rod and some bait, as if he wished he had never taken the office of sheriff.

Cayce said on a sudden tangent, "Luke, did you really like raising watermelons better than being sheriff?"

The sheriff gave him a startled look. "Well—the fact is I never raised watermelons. I just always thought I'd like to. Now what is it you want to do?"

"Arrange the work. Sam Williams can see to that. I want to talk to Aunt Blanche."

"What are you going to say to Miss Blanche?"

"I don't know. I guess I'm going to tell her she can stay here, it's her home. But I'm going to take that deed into court."

Luke moved absently along the pier looking down at the side where the fishing rods were left. There were no fishing rods then. At last he said, "I guess you'd better make some sort of arrangement with Miss Blanche. You'll have to fix it up so the groves are taken care of, you can't just walk off and leave them."

It was matter-of-fact, simple and logical, a mere statement of the atavistic knowledge of land and the care it requires.

"I'll not try to get away," Cayce said.

Luke became entirely an officer of the law. "It wouldn't do you any good to try to get away," he said crisply. "All right then, get busy. I'll pick you up in the morning."

He trudged back across the lawn and climbed wearily into his car. Cayce walked slowly to the house where Blanche waited for him. He wouldn't tell Blanche that he was, or would be in the morning, under arrest. Yet he didn't dare let himself hope that in the time the sheriff had given him, he could arrive at any evidence leading to the true facts of the judge's murder.

Blanche said, "What did the sheriff want?"

"Just to talk." He poured himself a drink. Even if he went to trial, they wouldn't convict him. But, of course, they could!

Blanche said, "We've got to get things clear between us. First," she locked her hands together and said earnestly, "I want you to forgive me."

It was the last thing Cayce had expected her to say. "Forgive you!"

"Yes. But it wasn't altogether my fault . . ." She checked herself and said, "Yes, it *was* my fault. I ought to have had more courage. More spirit. Your father expected me to take care of you, not only to see about your food and clothes and all that but take care of you like a mother. I didn't."

Her dark cloudy eyes looked misty as if there were tears in them. Cayce said, "But Aunt Blanche . . ."

"No, don't say anything. I've got to explain. Oh, I'm not

excusing myself, but you see, Cayce, I had some spirit in the beginning. It soon left me because it was easier to agree with my brother than to disagree. But I was cruel to you. I didn't mean to be but I was cowardly. I never took your part. I never stood between you and the judge. I'll have that on my conscience all my life, or would have had, if you hadn't left home and made a—" there was a warm, almost a proud note in her voice when she said, "made a man of yourself. Without him, without me, without anybody."

An odd sense of embarrassment caught Cayce; he didn't know what to say. He was the more perplexed because Blanche seemed again like a different woman, someone new and strange to him; it wasn't altogether the smart new dress, nor the trace of pink lipstick which was also new and startling on Blanche's lips.

She said, "Oh, Cayce, I was so weak, so foolish, but what else could I do? You could leave home, he drove you away. I'd have left, if I could, but where was I to go? I loved Ramon," she said suddenly.

Cayce thought, Ramon? Oh yes; that was her husband, divorced so long ago.

Blanche said dreamily as if looking back into the distant past, "Oh, we weren't getting along; we hadn't built our marriage yet. You know, you have to build a marriage like a house, brick by brick. But the judge—before I knew it, I was divorced and living here, keeping house for him. It was my own fault, I ought not to have let the judge influence me. I can't entirely blame the judge for that—except I *do* blame him," she said with sudden force. "I was under his influence always, the same as Lawrence, your father, always was; somehow we let the judge rule us just because he was stronger and more determined. Lawrence never got his eyes open to the judge. I did. But I didn't stop it when the judge talked Lawrence into writing in that life tenancy."

"The judge did that!"

"Of course. Lawrence intended to leave just a simple will, everything to you. It was the judge who thought of this unfair business of a deed and this life tenancy. Didn't you know that?"

"No!" How much that explained! "He wanted Blanchards."

"Certainly he wanted Blanchards. He hadn't anything else. Oh, he lent your father money when Lawrence bought this place. Surely you knew that. The judge made some money away back in the days of rum-running. Nobody ever really knew the truth about that. But later he established himself as a respectable citizen. Your father paid back the loan and fixed it so we could live here. My brother loved being called 'the judge.'" There was a weary scorn in Blanche's eyes. "He was called a fine, public-spirited man and—he was as cruel to me in all the subtle ways he could think of as he was cruel to you. You got out of it. I didn't." A shadow covered the new youthfulness in her face. "Roddy's no good. He's had one job after another. Finally the Velidas took him, just because his father was a Velidas, but Roddy—I'm afraid the judge was a bad example for him. He doesn't care how he gets money so long as he gets it. But it's not too late for Roddy. He's young. I'll save him in spite of himself. He's my son and I love him. But in a way, you're my son, too."

There was a long silence. It was as if the cool, half-shabby, comfortable and deeply familiar room was waiting and listening too. Finally Cayce said out of a vast astonishment, "I never knew you felt like this!"

Blanche leaned back against the chair. She said steadily, "I want you to forgive me, Cayce, not for anything I did to you but for all the things I didn't do because I didn't have the courage. I hated the judge. I've hated every day that I've spent here. The judge didn't tell me that I shared that life tenancy, and I know why. He wouldn't have yielded an ounce of his authority. Well, that's over. This place belongs to you." There was a long silence, yet for the first time between them an understanding silence. He believed her now. He believed every word she said.

He said at last, "It's your home, Aunt Blanche. I told you that. I meant it. . . ."

There were rapid footsteps on the porch. Roddy came in, gave Cayce and Blanche one swift, sharp glance, and said, "Sorry, I'm late to dinner."

They went in to dinner. Blanche talked with composure about nothing. Roddy's eyes were brilliant and active. Cayce, however, was only vaguely aware of that for he had so much to do and so much to think about; he was surprised when all at once dinner was over and Roddy was pulling out his mother's chair. Roddy followed his mother into the living room like a guard. He was alert and watchful, his dark eyes bright and determined. Belle had brought in the coffee tray before they left the table; it stood beside Blanche's chair and Cayce watched Blanche—this new Blanche—pour coffee into the little fragile cups.

He knew what Roddy wanted to say to his mother; he knew that Roddy would bring to bear every scrap of influence he had over Blanche. He is my son, Blanche had said;

and I love him; there would be a struggle between them and there was no way of guessing its outcome.

When the telephone rang it was like a sharp, compelling summons, jerking all three of them to swift attention. Cayce reached the study a few feet ahead of Roddy and answered it. And it was Dodie.

The busy country line was often blurred even between Blanchards and the Howard place; her voice was indistinct, high-pitched and unnatural. He could understand only a few words, ". . . I'll be there . . ."

"Where?" he shouted. "What do you mean . . ."

"The pier. At ten . . ." The telephone clicked and then began to buzz. He put it down.

"Who was that?" Roddy said sharply.

"Dodie. We were cut off."

"Aren't you going to call her back?" Roddy asked, his eyes alert.

He didn't answer. After a moment Roddy shrugged and went back to the living room. Cayce looked at his watch. It was twenty minutes to ten. He went out through the French doors and along the path beside the house.

Dodie, at least, still believed in him.

As he neared the corner of the house, through the open windows of the living room, he heard Roddy's voice, angry and demanding. He paused for a moment. Blanche replied; her words were not distinguishable but she sounded composed and firm. The night air was fragrant with jasmine. The clump of Melaleucas stood out, their gray trunks slender and ghostly.

He debated returning to the house and entering the discussion between Blanche and Roddy but all at once he was sure that Roddy could not, now, sway Blanche's decision. He strolled down toward the lake, leaving the lights of the house behind him. He rounded the black blotch of shadow that was the grove. The lake stretched out below, touched by starlight in silvery patches. It was barely light enough to see the pier. There were flying clouds, and as he waited, smoking and sitting on the pier, a heavy bank of clouds drifted halfway across the sky, like a curtain.

There must be, he thought, a wind high in the sky, sweeping the heavy clouds before it. Blanchards, and John's cottage and the groves all lay now in an enveloping darkness. The Burke place across the lake was still touched with starlight, and the lake, far out, glittered with silver.

Nothing moved anywhere. It was so still that he could hear

the faint whisper of water against the old pilings and the two boats, tied to the pier. He watched the bank of darkness advance, blotting out the silvery patches on the lake, until it swallowed up the Burke place and the swampland. There was something about that swift and steady advance that was threatening. He thought suddenly, Dodie ought not to be alone in that menacing blackness—as she had been the night before!

What a fool he had been to let her come!

Could he get to the Howard house before she left? The luminous little hands of his watch pointed to ten exactly. Would she come by the lake path—skirting the dense shadows of the grove?

He was starting for the path, to meet her, when he heard the tiny click of oarlocks from somewhere in the deep darkness, on the west side of the pier.

TWENTY-THREE

The pier quivered as he crossed it and leaned over. He saw the faint gleam of the boat and the light figure of a girl in the boat. It edged around the carpet of water hyacinths and nudged the pier, and Cayce said, "It's me," and leaned over to reach for the painter. He tied the boat. He was almost dizzy with relief. "I shouldn't have let you come. Last night . . ." He pulled her up out of the boat and into his arms.

And instantly all his senses telegraphed his mistake for it wasn't Dodie, it was Midge. She snuggled closely in his arms. "Cayce darling, I knew that really you felt like this. Of course, you couldn't say so. All that nonsense about being still married to Dodie! But that's not a real marriage and—" she gave a long complacent sigh, "Dodie will get that annulment. She promised me that."

He drew back abruptly. She waited a second, her face lifted toward him. Finally she said, "Why, Cayce, what's wrong?"

"I thought you were Dodie."

There was a small stiff silence. Then Midge said, "But Cayce, you always said I was your sweetheart. Ever since we were children. Then you went away and I waited and I waited for you and . . ."

"Midge," he said rather desperately, "you were engaged to Roddy."

"But I told you that—why, it just wasn't anything!"

"Midge—listen . . ."

148

"Well," she said after listening.

"Dodie's my wife," Cayce said, "and I love her."

"Oh," Midge said. Her voice sharpened. "Then why did you phone to me and ask me to meet you here?"

"What?"

"But you did! And I was so scared, Cayce. Rowing over here alone and in the dark. But I came because you asked me to and now you treat me like this. . . ."

"Midge, I didn't phone to you!"

"But you—the line was fuzzy, it always is sort of, but you said the pier at ten."

A sense of immediate danger came out of the still darkness. "Get in the boat. I'm going to take you home. Come on, Midge . . ."

For all her softness, Midge could be obstinate, but somehow he got her down into the boat again. Somebody had wanted him to be at the pier at ten; why? And why Midge?

Her small figure in its light dress faced him as he took the oars. Midge said after a moment, "Why are you so different, Cayce?"

He replied absently for he was thinking about a shadow on the pier behind Midge. Was it a man, or was it merely the long dim shadow of a piling? "People change. You're not in love with me, Midge. I can tell."

"Are you thinking about Roddy?"

He said, still absently, "Why didn't you marry Roddy?"

Midge gave a kind of little flounce. "If you want to know, it was the judge, the mean old thing."

That startled him. "The judge! I should think he'd have been all for it. Your father's got the biggest grove around here."

"Cayce," Midge said icily, "if you talk to me like that I'll get right out of this boat."

He grinned in spite of himself. The shadow on the pier had not moved so it wasn't a man, waiting there, listening—for what?

"What did the judge do?"

"Well if you really want to know," Midge said crossly, "he —pushed Roddy too much. He just kept after Roddy, telling him to marry me and that it was a good match and all that, and Roddy—well, you know—then Roddy wouldn't."

"It didn't exactly break your heart, did it?"

"You stop laughing, Cayce Clary. No," Midge said with candor. "No, it didn't break my heart but I was mad at the judge just the same."

"How did Roddy feel about it?"

149

"I don't care how Roddy felt! And you needn't think so much of Roddy's feelings. He made those footprints so they'd look like yours."

Cayce stopped rowing. "How did you know Roddy made those footprints?"

Midge said very sweetly and gently, "Because I saw him."

"*You saw him?*"

"Of course I did. I knew he was at home, it was around six and I wanted to see him. I thought he might take me to the club dance next week so I walked over to Blanchards. I saw Dodie in the pool but she didn't see me. I got into your driveway and there at the edge of the grove, I saw Roddy. He was sitting on the ground and had his shoes off and he was doing something to one foot. He looked so—queer somehow, that I just watched. And then he got up fast and went through the grove down toward the lake. He made those footprints, of course, and he remembered about the scar. . . ."

"How did he make those footprints?"

"Oh, that was easy. He had a roll of that black tape, adhesive tape. I think he got it out of his car. I guess he just stuck a little old leaf or twig or something under his foot."

So simple. "What did you do then?"

"I went back home. Dodie wasn't in the pool then. I guess she'd gone back to the house. Her radio was going when I went to my room. I just couldn't imagine what Roddy was up to. And then—then we heard about the judge. So I didn't tell anybody because I knew right away why Roddy had done that. He'd already found the judge and he was afraid they'd think maybe *he* had shot him so he just made it look as if it was you."

"But then—Zack must have told him that I was at home that afternoon."

"Roddy says he didn't. I—asked him. And I think Roddy was telling the truth. He said he didn't know you'd been at home until after Zack told the sheriff. So you see, he wasn't *really* trying to—to . . ."

"Incriminate me?"

"That's what I mean. Because you see he thought you were in New York and could prove it but—a sort of false clue—I mean a bare foot like that horrid Barefoot Deeler, and a scar like yours—well, nobody would suspect Roddy! It's perfectly clear. That is, to anybody who knows Roddy."

She was right about that. But Cayce was bewildered all the same. "Midge, didn't you know that as soon as they found out I was at home that afternoon, they did suspect me, and that footprint with a scar . . ."

She broke in. "Why, of course I knew it. But they aren't going to arrest you, Cayce! I'm not one bit worried about that."

Cayce swallowed hard, wondering how it would be to slap a woman, and started rowing again. "You didn't want to get Roddy into trouble. Is that it?"

He felt a slight vibration in the boat as if she wriggled. "Roddy's handsome. All the girls are after him. Besides he'll get some of the Velidas money. Oh, Cayce," she said plaintively, "why do you have to go and ask so many questions?"

He laughed unexpectedly and so loudly that it rang out over the water. "Midge—there's something you ought to know. Blanchards may not really belong to me, after all. Aunt Blanche has a life tenancy, too. Like the judge."

For a long time there was nothing but the dip and splash of his oars. At last Midge said, "Then that means that Miss Blanche is there as long as she lives and Roddy, too, doesn't it? Cayce," she said demurely, "I guess maybe I was mistaken thinking that you were still in love with me or that I was still in love with you. I guess, maybe I feel, well—just like a sister to you. I wouldn't for the world come between you and Dodie. And I can see now that you liked me as a sister. It was that all along."

He laughed again. Here were the mangroves; they glided into the deep shadow below them and the boat struck the concrete platform. "Everything's all right, Midge, and I'll try to be a brother to you. Now go up to the house and stay there. Tell Dodie to stay there."

He watched until he saw her figure outlined against the light from the house and the terrace door banged. Then he hurried along the driveway, across the road and into the long dark lane between the Australian pines. He grinned, thinking of Midge; she was cautious, trying to play it both ways; pretty and sweet and cautious and going to make the best market available.

When he reached the pier there was no one there. Somebody wanted him to be on that pier at ten o'clock. He wouldn't be there, but he'd be near it. He dropped down softly into the rowboat and waited.

The trouble was that nothing happened, except that after a long time somebody across the lake at the Burke place had a flashlight down at the edge of the lake. The flashlight jerked and wavered for a little while and then went out.

But somebody wanted him to be at the pier at a specific time. Somebody had telephoned to Midge, used Cayce's name and told her to be at the pier at the same time. Well then, who? And why?

Whoever it was, it was someone who knew and could count on—or artfully accentuate—the occasionally erratic and buzzing country line. Probably both telephone calls had been made by a man—it would be easier for a man to imitate a woman's voice than for a woman to imitate a man's voice. He had thought that Dodie's voice was strained and unnatural, but he had been so glad it was Dodie that he hadn't questioned it. Had that voice proclaimed itself as Dodie, or had Cayce merely jumped to the conclusion? It seemed to him, thinking back, that in the indistinct and blurred sounds, the word Dodie had clearly emerged. Whoever had telephoned to Midge had obviously told her it was himself, Cayce. Who, he thought again, and why?

It was easier to say who it was not. It was not Blanche, it was not Roddy who had telephoned to him. It wasn't Midge. It wasn't Dodie, he was certain of that. Well, then—who?

Nobody came along the pier. He would have heard the boards rattle no matter how stealthy a step. There was no sound at all from the lake. Why had someone wanted him, and Midge, to be there at exactly that time? Because something was going to happen. Well then, what? And why did it require Cayce's presence at the pier?

He was cramped and tired, waiting and listening. A dozen times he reached for a cigarette and stopped himself, for the light would betray his presence in the boat.

Time went on, in that stuffless darkness, while he surveyed the nebulous wall surrounding the judge's murder, seeking a revealing crevice. And at last, unexpectedly, he found it.

It was only a crevice. It was indeed only a repeated pattern. But there was a terrible and convincing logic about it.

He felt cold, on that hot night, as if his very heart had chilled. He wanted to escape that dreadful, supporting logic and he couldn't.

Yet there were two equally strong arguments against the ugly answer it gave him. One argument and an important one was that it provided no motive—no sound and strong motive for the judge's murder. *Unless a few words, carelessly spoken, carelessly heard, had a significance?* What significance he could not even guess.

He moved restlessly, shifting his cramped position in the boat. He looked out and across the black lake and saw a light in John's cottage.

Had John come back? Or was someone else there, surreptitiously exploring?

He untied the painter and began to row quickly toward the light. It was the only sign of life anywhere in that muted, heavy darkness. Yet all at once he felt that there was someone—something—on the lake with him. He stopped rowing and listened. There was nothing. Presently he began to row again. And then he heard a deep, barking grumble far off somewhere toward the swampland. So Old Stinker had returned.

Except for that the lake was a vast empty blackness. There was not a breath of motion, not a sound anywhere except the splash of his oars, yet again he stopped rowing to listen, struck sharply by that sense of someone or something near him.

At the same time he was surprised when suddenly his boat touched something gently.

It was another boat. He called softly, he didn't know why. "Who is it?"

As if for answer, the other boat bumped his sluggishly again. He dropped his oars, reached out and grasped the boat.

"Who is it?" he asked again but his voice caught, for one groping hand had discovered something. The boat was not empty.

He managed to secure it to his own boat with the painter. Then, reckless of the watching darkness, he lighted matches, one after the other.

At last he dropped the empty packet of matches into the lake. Old Stinker roared again, nearer this time. With feverish energy Cayce lashed the drifting, sluggish boat securely to his own and started back to the oars hard and fast. It was going to be a race with Old Stinker. The man in the rowboat had been stabbed. He was dead. It was Zack. And Old Stinker knew it, too.

It was hard rowing, pulling that heavy, horribly freighted boat behind him. Old Stinker was ominously silent, swimming swiftly through the black wake.

Here was the outline of John's boat landing. He pulled in beside it. He ought not to move Zack. He knew that, but he couldn't leave him in the boat either. He managed to secure both boats and ran through the dark winding path amid the bamboos. When he reached the lawn, lights from the porch spread across it. The sheriff was standing on the porch, staring downward. He ran up the steps and flung open the door. Then he saw John, sitting in the armchair, smoking.

Ten minutes later the three of them had hauled Zack's horribly heavy body up and across the landing strip.

Back in the cottage Luke used the telephone. "There'll be

153

some men here in a few minutes," he said, coming back into the porch. "I told you, Cayce, that I'd give you until morning. I can't now. I have to take you with me now, under arrest."

"Because of Zack?"

"Looks as if Zack knew more than he told me about the judge's murder, and tried to blackmail you. Yes, because of Zack and the judge."

"But I told you about Zack. I brought him here. Old Stinker was on his way. Nobody would ever have know what happened to Zack."

"I'd have known," the sheriff said simply. "That's why I'm here. Zack left his car in the grove leading into the Burke place. Mr. Burke found it there and phoned to me. He said that he had seen a flashlight down at his landing and he went down and one of his boats was missing. I started out to find Zack, I knew he'd be on the lake somewhere—and then I saw John's light."

"We were afraid you'd been killed, John," Cayce said.

"I'm sorry. That never occurred to me. I was hiding out in Tampa—trying to find some of the judge's old cronies or get some kind of line on somebody he had known during his rum-running days. Seemed to me—well, I thought it might help. But I couldn't find anybody that knew anything. . . ."

"I could have told you that, John," the sheriff broke in. "That whole outfit was scattered years ago."

Cayce said to the sheriff, "Those footprints *were* faked."

"Oh, sure. My guess is that Roddy did it. You see, he said he went out to find the judge, didn't find him and came back. But he said, too, that the judge hadn't gone fishing. If Roddy had gone clear down to the pier, he'd have seen the judge—couldn't have missed him. Remember, he was looking for him. Roddy had read that newspaper story about Barefoot Deeler. He remembered the scar on your foot. Guess he was scared, thought somebody might accuse him; he knew about all that money in the judge's name and that, he figured, would be considered a motive."

"He didn't know that I'd been there that afternoon. At least that's what Midge says."

"Well, I don't reckon he did. If you were in New York, as he thought you were, the scar on the footprints wouldn't do you any harm. Not that Roddy would care about that. But he was scared and he worked fast and did the only things he could think of to turn suspicion from him." He paused. Already there was the sound of an automobile engine racing furiously in the distance. "I've got to put handcuffs on you, Cayce."

"Luke—will you give me a little more time?"

"I gave you time. You know how to shoot. You knew how to knife a man so fast and hard that he didn't know it was coming . . . Oh, blast," Luke said, fumbling at his belt. "Left the handcuffs in my car. You stay right here, Cayce. Don't make a move." The door slammed behind him.

The car was coming rapidly along the winding road, nearer and nearer the cottage. It stopped, doors banged, somebody shouted, "Luke . . ."

Cayce went to the screen. The men were running down to the lake. Their light shirts flashed past; their excited questions and speculations came in a hubbub to his ears. Then they disappeared in the black patch of bamboos.

There wasn't time; there wasn't time for anything. But it had to be done. "Have you got any money, John?" he said.

"Money! About two hundred. *What for?*"

"Get out," Cayce said. He couldn't look at John.

There was an instant of silence. Then John said, "What are you talking about?"

"Oh, John!" Cayce turned to face him. John was sitting coolly, watching him. "There's no time for all this. Get out while you can. The men are down there and you can take your car and . . ."

"Why, Cayce, are you saying that I killed the judge?"

All right, then, Cayce thought; lay it on the line. "Listen, John. Zack must have told you that he'd seen you out on the lake in your boat a long time before you admitted to being out there and finding the judge. Dodie saw your boat—or part of it. You saw her. She sat on the landing and you couldn't get away until she'd gone swimming. The day of the inquest—sometime—Zack told you he'd seen you. Maybe he was lying and maybe he wasn't but you couldn't be sure. So you told him to come at night and you'd talk to him—or pay him off. He came—but you'd left the cottage; probably you couldn't decide just what to do. You heard me and Dodie. You followed us up to the cottage and—maybe hid out there in the shrubbery, close to the porch. You heard Dodie say that she *did* remember something. So you had to get rid of Dodie—and you had to get rid of Zack, to be safe."

John's face was a tight gray mask. "Dodie wasn't killed."

"That's what I'm trying to remember—I'm trying to believe —that, really, you couldn't kill her. You tried to but you couldn't. *John—don't you see I know?*"

"Cayce—this is all—speculation. Why, you wouldn't accuse me of murder!"

"I tell you there's no time for this, John. They'll be back

155

here in a few minutes. When you killed the judge you thought I'd have an alibi—I'd be on the plane, nobody could accuse me. When you knew the police were searching for you and they'd find you, you decided to come back and kill Zack. I don't know how you got him to take a boat—probably told him you'd got hold of some money and would pay him off, something like that. And then—you tried to fix it so I'd have an alibi again. So you phoned to me and phoned to Midge. Midge—not Dodie—because you knew that Dodie was still married to me and couldn't testify. Nobody but you and the sheriff knew that. Now—get your money and get out, John. There's nothing I can do for you."

John sat back in his chair. "Why should I murder the judge? I wanted you to come home, Cayce, sure. But a man's not going to stick his head in a noose for somebody else no matter how much . . ."

"Oh, John, believe me! *I know*. You killed your wife, didn't you? And let it out to the judge sometime—maybe when you'd been drinking."

John's lips were gray now; they moved stiffly. "That was an accident. Everybody knows it was an accident and a—tragedy that changed my whole life."

"It changed your life because after you'd killed her you wished you hadn't. Remorse—fear—guilt—I don't know what. Maybe you didn't really mean to kill her." Cayce felt a terrible weariness; he was right. "The judge would have held that over your head all your life. He wouldn't have reported it to the police; maybe he wasn't sure that they could prove it; maybe he couldn't get enough of the story out of you. Maybe he liked to taunt you with it, show his power. But he *knew*—and you knew that he knew. You tried twice to kill him—ways that would look like an accident—the alligator, the oleanders. Nothing worked. So you shot him."

John stared at him, his eyes bright and wary. "If the judge told anybody that, he was—he was lying. Malicious and . . ."

Lay it on the line, Cayce thought again. "You needled the judge about my property. He said that he didn't want a man with your history in his house. He had the stronger argument, John."

"My history . . ."

"The thing that changed your life, the important thing that you couldn't escape, was your wife's death. When I thought of that, there seemed to be a link. You see—if it had been an accident you might have blamed yourself, but you'd have realized that it *was* an accident. It wouldn't have haunted you as it has, all these years." He listened for the men coming back from the lake; perhaps there was still time. "I'll have to tell Luke. He'll get after the police in your home town. . . ."

John rose. "All right. You've got me. They called it accidental but—they weren't sure about it. Once Luke goes to them . . ." He paused. A kind of surprise came into his face. "In a way it *was* an accident, Cayce! There was another man. . . . I tried to stop it—she laughed at me. I was driving— I saw a chance to run the car over a ravine and before I thought twice about it—well, that's what I did. I jumped out —the car went over. It happened just like that. All at once. I didn't—really mean to kill her—I didn't plan it. They questioned me and questioned me but they had to let me go. The judge deserved what he got. But I wouldn't have hurt you, Cayce. I thought I'd fixed it so you'd never be suspected. . . ."

"You were going to let the sheriff arrest me."

John turned away. "I was going to confess. That is, if they arrested you or—or anybody else. But when the time came— I couldn't. Murder changes a man. It's as if you were two men—one of them yourself, living like other people. The other one, deep down, is the murderer and—that man is different. He's another man. . . ."

The sheriff opened the door and came in. "I heard everything. I thought you'd break down, John—after you knew I was going to arrest Cayce. That's why I told you I was going to arrest you this afternoon, Cayce. I figured you might be in touch with John and you'd tell him. But I thought when he heard that he'd come clean. I've got evidence, John."

John didn't move. The sheriff had a gun in his hand; his face was moist and his eyes steely. "Cayce," he said, without looking away from John. "How many boats at your place? Two. How many boats at the Howard place? Three. How many boats at the Burke place? Two. And John has one boat."

John moistened his lips. "What's that got to do with it?"

"I went out to MacDill again this afternoon. I knew that boat that Dodie saw was worrying her. She's always liked you, John—felt sorry for you, I guess. Well—young Bill Burke was in one of those bomber crews. When he went over the lake, of course, he looked down. He knows the lake. They went fast but he spotted the boats and counted them, too. There were two at the Burke place—three at the Howard's— *three at Blanchards—and none here.*"

John said, "I'll be back in a minute . . ." and walked into the cottage.

Cayce started after him. Luke's hand clamped down on his

arm. "Better this way," Luke said, listening. "It may cost me my job. But I'd rather raise watermelons anyway."

"*Luke* . . ." He tried to wrench his arm away but the sheriff gripped hard, watched the door into the cottage and said in a kind of mumble, filling in the silence with words, "Guess he had an extra gun—no license for it. Dropped it in the lake. Dropped the knife there, too. But I couldn't figure out *why* he killed the judge . . ." The shot came then, rocking the cottage and the black, quiet night. It was an accurate shot. Cayce was thankful for that.

He was dimly aware of men running into the cottage. Luke put his hand on Cayce's shoulder. "Get up, boy. Go home. It's best this way. . . ."

But once more in the boat, rowing through the blackness of the lake with the lights in John's cottage getting farther and farther away, Cayce stopped rowing and let the boat drift. It seemed tragically ironic that John the murderer had been in fact trapped by the John whom Cayce knew; it he hadn't tried to make sure that Cayce had a perfect alibi for Zack's murder—as he had believed that Cayce had an alibi for the time of the judge's murder, the oddity of that repeated pattern would not have struck Cayce with its terrible logic. And if the John whom Cayce had known had not tried to defend Cayce's interests with the judge, the judge would not have retaliated by threatening John, the murderer, with silky, taunting hints: "A man with your history . . ." It was like the judge to use his knowledge that way; it had the judge's stamp.

After a long time he began to row toward Blanchards. Dodie was waiting for him at the fishing pier. "I saw the light in John's cottage . . ."

He took her tight in his arms. She waited a moment; he heard her quickly drawn breath before she whispered, "Was it John?"

He told her all of it, the whole story; he told her again, relieving his heart, certain of her understanding.

"You had to do it," she said at last. "John was right when he said it was as if he were two men. It was another man, not the John we knew, who was the murderer. It's in the past now, Cayce."

Above them the lights from the house—his home, Dodie's home—shone with a tranquil, welcoming glow. "You're my wife, Dodie. Come home with me now."

The lake whispered softly below. A breath from the jasmine came through the night air. Dodie said simply, "Why, of course I'm your wife. Take me home."